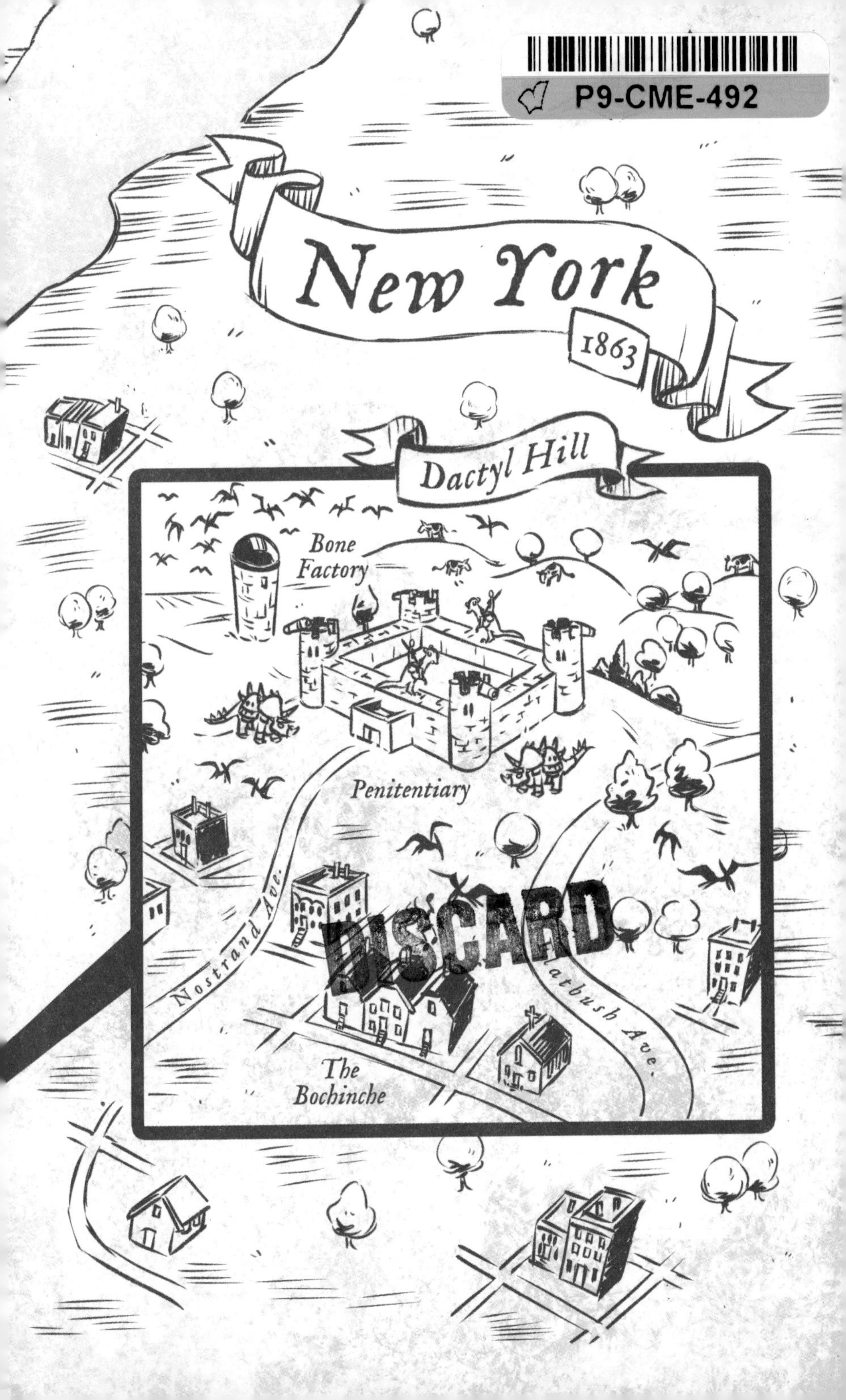
New York
1863
Dactyl Hill
Bone Factory
Penitentiary
Nostrand Ave.
latbush Ave.
The Bochinche

Praise for

DACTYL HILL SQUAD

"Daniel has imagined the unimaginable and in doing so sends readers on a dino thrill ride. I have been talking about this book nonstop! The kids, the dinosaurs, the Civil War, this book is true fire. It is everything I didn't even know I needed." – Jacqueline Woodson, National Ambassador for Young People's Literature

"An extraordinary adventure full of heart and imagination that adults will enjoy reading just as much as kids! This is the story that would've made me fall in love with reading when I was a kid." – Tomi Adeyemi, #1 *New York Times* bestselling author of *Children of Blood and Bone*

"In this Tyrexcellent historical realignment – fast paced, but deceptively packed with amazing detail – Older's uprising of sheroes and heroes grips, stomps, and soars from start to finish." – Rita Williams-Garcia, *New York Times* bestselling author of *One Crazy Summer*

"*Dactyl Hill Squad* is an engaging, lively adventure with a heroine I wish I were, in a world I didn't want to leave."
—Jesmyn Ward, two-time National Book Award-winning author of *Sing, Unburied, Sing*

"This incredible story brings history to life with power, honesty, and fun." — Laurie Halse Anderson, *New York Times* bestselling author of *Chains*

"A crackling fantasy adventure full of thrilling scenes."
—James McPherson, Pulitzer Prize-winning author of the *Battle Cry of Freedom*

"As a historian of New York City, I'm thrilled with Daniel José Older's melding of the best of history and fantasy in *Dactyl Hill Squad*. I couldn't put it down! It was wonderful to see familiar people, places, and events in fantastic but still humanly true circumstances. What a perfect way to introduce history to a new generation of readers — I can't wait to share this book with my nephews. Thank you, Daniel José Older!" — Leslie Harris, author of *In the Shadow of Slavery*

DANIEL JOSÉ OLDER
DACTYL HILL SQUAD
BOOK ONE
ARTHUR A. LEVINE BOOKS
AN IMPRINT OF SCHOLASTIC INC.

Library of Congress Control Number: 2018016850
ISBN 978-1-338-26881-2
10 9 8 7 6 5 4 3 2 1 18 19 20 21 22

Printed in the U.S.A. 23
First edition, September 2018

Book design by Christopher Stengel

FOR CALYX AND PAZ

TABLE OF CONTENTS

• PART ONE •
THE RAPTOR CLAW

CHAPTER ONE
OUT THE DOOR AND AWAY

"MARGARET!"

Magdalys Roca sat on her bed in the girls' bunk at the Colored Orphan Asylum and closed her eyes. Her day satchel was packed, her uniform was on, shoes buckled; she'd wrestled her hair into a tight bun the way the matrons insisted she do. The triceratops wagon was leaving any second for the theater, and the theater was just about the best place to be as far as Magdalys was concerned.

But . . .

"Margaret Rocheford, come here this instant!"

She had sworn, *sworn!* to herself that she wouldn't answer to that name anymore. She would answer to her *real* name, the way her brother Montez said it, the way her long-gone sisters had: *Magdalys* with that *y* drawn out long and sharp *eeeees*, like a melody.

The matron's footsteps clack-clacked up the marble hall, paused, and then turned with a squeak and headed away again.

When Montez was there and he did say her name like the song she knew it to be, she didn't really care what Miss Henrietta Von Marsh called her. But now he was gone too, gone six weeks and two days to be exact, and sure the other kids called her Magdalys (and Maggie, Mags, or Mag-D, depending on the day), but it wasn't the same; it was a stumble not a song, and she certainly wouldn't be responding to Margaret. And Rocheford even less. So Magdalys sat there, and she tried not to think of the show she would miss at the Zanzibar Savannah Theater.

"The trike wagon will just leave without you, I suppose," Von Marsh called out as the hallway double doors squeaked open. "Shame, really. I heard the Crunks are performing *The Tempest* tonight." And then the doors slammed shut and the clack-clacking got quieter and quieter.

The Tempest! It wasn't Magdalys's favorite Shakespeare play, but she'd read it (she'd read most of them) and she was instantly filled with wonder: How would Halsey and Cymbeline Crunk, the two lead actors of the only all-black Shakespearean company in New York, bring that story of exiled wizards and lovers and monsters to life? Who would play which role and how would they do the beast Caliban and what kinds of stage dinos would they use and how would the rowdy crowd react and . . .

Dang it! Magdalys thought, jumping to her feet and grabbing her satchel. She wasn't going to let Von Marsh's stubbornness make her miss out on some good theater. She shoved open the door and blitzed down the brightly lit corridor, her footfalls echoing all around her.

A bunch of kids were studying and playing board games in the first floor common area. "Whoa," Bernadette and Syl yelled as Magdalys blew past. "Slow down, Speeds McGee!" Sweety Mae called after her. But Magdalys didn't have time to stop and banter. She wasn't going to make it, and then she'd be mad at herself all night, and her already bad mood would sink beneath the floorboards as she imagined all the fun Two Step and Mapper and Little Sabeen were having without her.

"Careful now," old Mr. Calloway called when Magdalys slammed open the front doors and rocketed down the big, fancy staircase. "I just mopped!" Magdalys slowed a bit so she wouldn't slip and splatter herself all over the stone walking path ahead. Mr. Calloway had escaped a provisional farm in upstate New York long before Magdalys was born, and she tried to be as nice to him as she could.

"Sorry, Mr. Calloway!" she called over her shoulder. "See you tomorrow!"

"Alright!" Mr. Calloway called back.

Up ahead, Varney, the orphanage's huge old triceratops,

grunted and stomped his feet. Great big folds of flesh hung down from his massive belly and dangled in dollops over each other along his four thick legs. The two horns poking out from his forehead were dull and his sleepy eyes had bags under them, but Varney still managed to make the supply runs twice a week and take the kids on field trips to the theater now and then. In the orphanage library's tattered edition of *The Field Guide to North American Dinos, Pteros & Other Assorted -Sauria* (which everyone just called the Dinoguide), Dr. Barlow Sloan described triceratopses as *noble and docile beasts who wanted nothing more than to sit around chewing on grass and leaves all day, but were perfectly willing to ride into battle and march for weeks on end if called upon to do so by their masters.*

Magdalys always wished she could spend more time with Varney. Dinos were much better than humans, mostly. They didn't make up names for you or judge you for how you wore your hair — they just lumbered around eating and pooping and carrying people places.

But it was only a few years ago that New York had passed a law granting black citizens the right to dinoride, and white people in Manhattan still bristled and stared when they saw someone with brown skin astride those massive scaly backs. Magdalys had no idea why anyone would want to keep her from dinoriding just because of the color of her skin, but she knew the orphanage certainly wouldn't let any of its wards near any dinos, except Varney, and him only every once in a while.

So Magdalys mostly had to be content with watching the great beasts cavort along outside her window: The lamplighter's iguanodons would pass first thing in the morning, extinguishing the lanterns as the day broke. Then the commuter brachys would stomp past, passengers cluttered on the saddles and hanging from straps along the side. By noon the streets would fill with stegosaurs lugging supplies and the duckbill riders in fancy dress clothes, heading off to important meetings, while microraptors scurried across the roads, carrying messages or making nuisances of themselves. Most of the trikes and raptors had been sent down south to fight the Confederates, but every once in a while she'd see one of those too. Magdalys could watch them out her window all day, but it wasn't the same as being out there with the dinos.

"Heeyah!" Marietta Gilbert Smack called out, and Varney heaved forward, pulling the wagon hitched to his back into motion.

No! Magdalys thought, sprinting through the big ornate gates enclosing the orphanage. A stitch opened up in her side. *Wait!*

Varney stopped with a snort and sigh. He turned his big horned head and directed a single droopy eye at Magdalys. Magdalys skidded to a halt. Had Varney somehow . . . ? It couldn't be. The old trike blinked once, then seemed to nod at her. Magdalys gasped.

"Mags!" Two Step yelled.

"Magdalys!" Little Sabeen squealed. "You made it!"

"So you decided to accept your name after all, *Margaret*," Henrietta Von Marsh said, a smug smile sliding across her face.

"No." Magdalys grabbed Two Step's outstretched hand and heaved herself onto the wagon. "I decided to go to the theater with my friends."

"Hold the wagon, Marietta," Von Marsh said with a withering scowl. She glared at Magdalys, who had made herself comfortable on the bench beside Two Step and Little Sabeen. "Young lady, when I call your name, I expect you to answer."

"I will answer," Magdalys said. "When you call my *real* name."

"Your *real* name is Margaret. Period. Your" — she curled up her lips in distaste — "*other* name no longer applies."

Magdalys took a deep breath, willing herself not to unleash the volcano fire of rage she had bubbling up inside her. *Can't we just go,* she thought, half hoping old Varney had somehow really heard her a few moments ago, half feeling like she was completely bonkers for even thinking that. *Go . . .*

"That is a remnant of the life you left behind," Von Marsh went on. "A life, I might add, that you don't even remember. You're in America now, not Cuba. And you will present yourself in American society as a proper little colored girl, as long as you are under my roof."

Varney grumbled like a tired old man and then heaved forward, pulling the wagon out of the driveway and onto Fifth

Avenue. "Hold the trike, I said, Marietta!" Von Marsh hollered, nearly toppling from the sudden lurch of movement.

"Good thing," Magdalys muttered as they rumbled out into the early evening streets of Manhattan, "we're not under your roof."

CHAPTER TWO
CITY OF WHISPERS

THE DINO LISTENED *to me,* Magdalys thought as Varney stomped along downtown toward the neighborhood everyone called the Raptor Claw, where the Zanzibar Savannah Theater was. He'd done just what she'd told him to. *Twice!* Magdalys had heard people talk about an ancient race of dinoriding warriors who could communicate with their steeds, but everyone knew that was all myth and rumor (Dr. Barlow Sloan, in particular, dedicated a whole side column of the Dinoguide to harrumphing the idea). And even if *were* true, it was ages ago, not today, in New York City. Certainly not some random orphan kid, right? It had to be coincidence.

Still, the nagging feeling that something extraordinary had just happened persisted . . .

"Watch this," Two Step said, standing in the middle of the wobbling cart and lifting both his wide arms to the sky. "I got a new move!"

"Oh, do sit down, young man," Old Mother Virginia Brimworth chided. "If you fall and hurt yourself we'll never hear the end of it from trustees."

Magdalys rolled her eyes. No one listened to Old Brimworth, and she usually got distracted so quickly after saying anything that it didn't matter anyway. "Do it!" Magdalys called. On the bench across from her, Amaya was staring out into the city around them, a sullen frown painted across her face, brow furrowed. Amaya always looked kind of sullen, and she didn't talk to too many people, but now there was something else: She looked alert.

Two Step spun once, then slid all the way to one side of the cart and made his whole body undulate like a wave. Then he jumped, clapped twice over his head, and did the whole thing again.

"Good heavens!" Old Brimworth grumbled.

"Brilliant!" Mapper yelled as Sabeen and Magdalys burst into applause.

"Again," Sabeen demanded. Amaya just stared at the old shacks and rowhouses of the darkening city around them. What was she watching for?

Magdalys closed her eyes, tuned into the wagon wheels rumbling through muddy cobblestone streets beneath her, the rocking cart, Varney's grunts and plodding footfalls, Sabeen and Mapper's laughter as Two Step fell into another round of dancing.

Something was different about the city on this warm July evening, and Magdalys couldn't put her finger on what it was.

"What's wrong?" Two Step asked, panting as he slid onto the bench beside her. A few lights flickered in the windows around them, but not many. Two Step was the one orphan Magdalys had come to think of as a friend. The others — she looked out for them when she could, especially Little Sabeen, and she had a good time with Bernadette and Syl, and Mapper sometimes. But the truth about orphan life was this: Nothing ever stayed the same. You made friends only to have them ripped away one bright morning with no reason given. They would just be gone. And if not all the sudden, they'd age out at seventeen and get shipped somewhere else anyway. And if they didn't, in five more years Magdalys herself would. So why bother?

Still, Two Step seemed to understand her without her ever having to speak, and that was the closest thing to friendship she could imagine. He had light brown skin and a big fro that he constantly argued with the matrons about, and a big belly that jiggled up and down when he laughed and big arms that felt safe when they wrapped around Magdalys for a hug. But he'd be gone one day too.

Just like Magdalys's sisters, Julissa and Celia.

Just like Montez.

"I don't know," Magdalys said, shivering against the

sudden night breeze. "It's . . ." She listened for a moment, tried to pick up something beyond the wagon wheels and clomping dino. Besides the far-off hoots of some sauropods, there was nothing. Nothing at all. "That's it," she whispered.

"What?" Two Step said, squinting out into the darkness. "I don't hear anything."

"Exactly!" Magdalys said. On a normal summer night, Manhattan sizzled with hollers, guffaws, and arguments, a million tidbits of gossip that warbled and bassooned down alleyways and over rooftops, across bustling avenues and through dingy saloons, back out into the streets where they were chewed on until all the juice was extracted, and then discarded to make room for the next morsel. Farmers and fishmongers would be packing up for the night, cursing and haranguing each other by way of saying see you tomorrow, and various merchants would be standing outside their stores, waiting for that one last customer to round out the day's sales. Dinos of all shapes and sizes should've been trundling down the throughway, skittering across intersections, hauling cargo along for a late delivery at some grocer or apothecary.

Instead, a single iguanodon limped along the cobblestones, its hunchbacked rider reaching a long pole up to light the street lanterns one by one. Magdalys watched him as they passed. His hands were shaking, and he kept looking around like at any moment something might jump out of the shadows and devour him. Amaya was staring at him too, and then she turned her wide eyes to Magdalys, as if to confirm they'd both noticed the same thing. Magdalys nodded ever so slightly.

"You think something's about to happen?" Two Step asked, not bothering to pretend he wasn't scared.

Magdalys nodded, then shrugged. "Sure seems like it." She liked that Two Step didn't feel like he had to keep up some pretense of bravery around her. It seemed like this strange, almost silent city kept whispering something under its breath, just a notch too quiet to make out, and Magdalys had no idea what secrets the night was hiding.

"A dactyl came with some grams today, children," Von Marsh announced. She pulled a stack of envelopes from her purse. "Kyle Tannery." Mapper hopped up, excited, and grabbed his letter, tearing it open before he'd even gotten back to the bench. "Sabeen Raymond." Von Marsh handed the letter to Two Step, who passed it to Sabeen. "Amaya Trent." Amaya didn't move, just stared at the passing city. "Amaya? You don't want your letter? It's from the General, I believe." Von Marsh adjusted her spectacles and tried to hold the envelope still amidst the bumping of the wagon. "Yes, the General." She looked up.

Amaya didn't answer, but her eyes looked wider than Magdalys had ever seen them.

Von Marsh sighed. "Very well then." She glanced at the last envelope, scowled. "Margaret Rocheford."

Now it was Magdalys's turn to sit perfectly still and gaze off into the distance. But still . . . a letter! Who could it be from?

"Margaret Rocheford," Von Marsh said again, this time with that shrill snarl she used to make a point.

Magdalys didn't remember much about her sisters. All four Roca kids been dropped off at the Colored Orphan Asylum when Magdalys was just a baby. Julissa and Celia spoke Spanish to her and combed her hair and said her name like a song, and Magdalys recognized her eyes in theirs. And then one day when Magdalys was four, a mustached man who reeked of tobacco appeared and took Julissa and Celia back to Cuba with no explanation, leaving just Magdalys and Montez. Magdalys had cried and cried and Montez, then only a kid himself, had tried to comfort her, but she could tell he was barely holding it together, so they ended up sobbing themselves to sleep on the common room sofa, where Mr. Calloway had put a blanket on them and convinced everyone to just leave them be instead of hustling them off to the bunks.

And six weeks ago, Montez had announced that he was leaving. "I have to do my part," he said, looking about as terrified and distraught as Magdalys felt inside. "Even though we weren't born here, this war will determine what happens to me, to you — to all of us. I have to do my part. I can't just sit here while it all happens hundreds of miles away."

So, not just leaving: Montez was joining the Union Army. Montez who was skinny and wore big glasses and hated fighting and loved reading, Montez who still cried sometimes when he talked about Julissa and Celia, and always helped out the younger kids, Montez was off to war, and Magdalys was alone.

Well, as alone as one could be in the midst of almost two hundred orphans and semiorphans between the ages of one and seventeen.

If the letter was from Montez, that changed everything, and Henrietta Von Marsh knew it. Magdalys finally exhaled in defeat and turned to face her. "Who . . . who's it from?"

"Oh," the matron declared, the slightest hint of a gloating smile curving her thin lips, "you're Margaret now?"

Magdalys narrowed her eyes. "What's the name on the envelope?"

Von Marsh looked perturbed for a moment, then simply shook her head. "I'm not going over this with you again, young lady."

Magdalys tried to contain the wrath burning through her. "Who . . . is . . . my gram . . . from?"

"If you had really wanted to know," Von Marsh chortled, "you would've answered when I called you the first time." She patted her purse once and then turned away. "Now you'll just have to wait till after the little play to find out, I suppose."

Magdalys launched across the cart. Her hands reached out toward Von Marsh; she would tackle her and she would get her stinking letter. The other orphans were standing, eyebrows raised, mouths opening, and then a strange grunting sound erupted in Magdalys's head: *Ree rooh arroooh* it went, and it sounded frantic, terrified. Magdalys froze. She looked around. Everyone was staring at her; no one seemed to notice the increasingly shrill squeals.

"Uh . . . Magdalys?" Two Step said.

"Didn't anyone else hear that?" Magdalys said.

Sabeen looked scared. "Hear wha —" she started to say, but then a sharp voice called out, "Stop there, you!" and the squeal in Magdalys's head became a shriek: *AREEEE-OOOHH!!* Magdalys ducked just as Varney reared up, jolting the cart to a sudden halt.

CHAPTER THREE
KNUCKLESKULL CHECKPOINT

HAD MAGDALYS SOMEHOW heard the dino get spooked? Inside her head? It certainly seemed like it . . . No one else had seemed to notice at all, and now, she realized, they were all staring at something just above her.

A knuckleskull loomed its ugly face over the wagon. Uneven bony growths made the dino's head look like a clenched fist with a snout poking out. It was reared all the way up on its huge hind legs, shorter forelimbs pawing idly against the wood planks.

Dr. Barlow Sloan spent a whole chapter of the Dinoguide trashing knuckleskulls. *Ugly, irrelevant, useless, lazy, good-for-nothing, abrupt, flatulent,* and *petulant* were some of the choice adjectives he'd selected for them. Magdalys had no idea how a dino could be relevant, let alone irrelevant, or whether one species would really be more prone to dinofarts than another, but either way, it seemed like Dr. Sloan was having a bad day when he wrote that entry.

The dino blinked twice, then wheezed and snorted, eyeing the orphans. Its rider, a helmeted police officer with an unpleasant frown, growled at Marietta: "What business have you with these colored children in the city tonight?"

"Why, I don't see how our business is any business of yours," Marietta snapped. She was the youngest matron and the only one that seemed to actually talk to the orphans instead of at them.

"Ah, Officer," Von Marsh tittered, hurrying to the front of the cart. "Pay no mind to Marietta. She's quite fiery, you know. We're simply taking them to the theater, young sir . . ."

Magdalys saw Sabeen wrap her small hand around Amaya's and squeeze. Mapper and Two Step stood perfectly still, hands at their sides.

"Well, this isn't a good night to be out" — the officer shifted his mouth around like he was chewing on the words some before he spat them out — "with their likes." He nodded at Magdalys, Two Step, Mapper, Amaya, and Sabeen. Magdalys felt her stomach sink. *Whatever the cop's talking about must be why the city's so creepy quiet,* she thought. And then: *No theater* . . . It felt ridiculous to care about missing out on a play when the whole night seemed so full of danger, but the menacing city only made Magdalys even hungrier to disappear into some fantasy world.

"I'm afraid I don't understand what you're saying, young man," Von Marsh said. "I am Henrietta Von Marsh of the Ladies' Manumission Society, and these children are wards of the Colored Orphan Asylum. Now if you don't mind, we'll be on our way . . ."

Magdalys wasn't sure if that little speech was supposed to settle the matter somehow, but the officer was clearly unmoved. "Lady, haven't you been paying attention? This whole city's about to —"

"That's enough, Officer," a voice snapped. The knuckle-skull and the cop both startled and then hopped to attention. Varney let out a concerned wheeze and stomped his feet. All five orphans leaned up against the far rail of the wagon to see who had spoken.

A middle-aged white man with a clipped, sallow face stood looking up at them. Tufts of white hair sprouted from either side of his otherwise bald head like some distraught nebulous fungi. A shiny medallion punctuated his long black magistrate robes: a roaring tyrannosaurus inside a circle with some writing around it that Magdalys couldn't make out.

"Magistrate Riker, sir," the officer said. "I didn't know you were out and about tonight. I was just warning these matrons abou —"

"That's *enough,* I said." Riker's voice was quiet but razor-sharp. The officer shut up accordingly.

Magdalys took a step back as Riker walked a slow, deliberate strut toward the back of the wagon. "Now, Miss

Henrietta Von Marsh — of the Ladies' Manumission Society, is it?"

Henrietta Von Marsh just stared at him for a few moments. Riker mounted the wagon in a single, smooth movement, almost like he was more liquid than man. Magdalys felt herself recoil inside but tried not to let it show on her face. "Is it?" he said again.

"Ah, quite," Von Marsh sputtered. "Indeed. Yes."

"And Miss Von Marsh of the Ladies' Manumission Society, I believe I overheard you say you're going to the *theater*." The magistrate drawled the word out with a soft lilt. "How charming. And I presume you have paperwork for all these" — he scrunched up his face like he'd just swallowed a slightly turned piece of fruit — "children."

Von Marsh cocked her head. "Paperwork?"

"To prove that they're not fugitive slaves, of course. You know we've had terrible trouble with that these days: contraband. It's illegal to harbor fugitives, particularly in a time of war."

"Why, Magistrate!" Von Marsh scoffed. "That's not true! But I assure you, these are free children and not fugitive slaves in the least! I give you my word as a member of one of the noblest families of New York City."

"Alas," Magistrate Riker sighed, "without proper papers, I'm afraid we'll have to take the children into the custody of the city."

"Custody of the city?" Marietta gasped. "You mean prison?"

Panic seized Magdalys. *Prison?* And then what? She'd heard stories of black New Yorkers vanishing off the streets, never to be seen again. Folks said they'd been snatched up and sent down south into slavery. Would she survive plantation life? Up front, Varney whinnied and snorted, sending tremors through the wagon. Magdalys didn't know if it was her terror seeping into the dino or his own, but either way she wanted out of there.

Riker smiled. "Prison is such an ugly word, don't you think?"

She had no idea if she could actually get the dino to do what she wanted, but even if she did, then what? A tired old trike couldn't outrun a knuckleskull. And cops had guns. Not to mention whatever untold horrors lay in wait deeper in the city tonight.

Still — if she couldn't get Varney to make a run for it, at least she could cause a distraction. *Up, Varney,* Magdalys thought. *Rear up!*

Varney immediately squealed and raised his front legs into the air, lifting the cart and sending the knuckleskull stumbling backward. Everyone grabbed the rails to steady themselves.

"Oh dear!" Old Brimworth cried, just waking up from what must've been a very pleasant nap. "What in heavens is going on?"

"You, girl," the cop snapped at Marietta. "Control this trike."

"I'm trying," Marietta said.

So am I, Magdalys thought.

Riker's glare landed on Magdalys. His eyes narrowed, like he was shooting beams of light out of them directly into her soul. Could he tell what she was trying to do? Magdalys stared back at him. *Easy, Varney,* she thought. *Shhhhh.* And Varney settled with a snort and a grumble.

"I see," Riker said softly, a smile creasing his lips. "I see."

"What's that?" Von Marsh asked.

Riker whirled around, suddenly magnanimous. "Nothing at all, dear lady. Which theater was it you said you were attending?"

Magdalys shuddered. Everything in her wanted to be away from this horrible man.

"Why, the Zanzibar Savannah, of course," Von Marsh said, blinking.

"Ah, of course, of course, excellent." Riker slid his icy gaze along each of their faces, stopping once again on Magdalys. "And what is this unfortunate creature's name?"

"That is Miss Margaret Rocheford, twelve years old, Magistrate, but I fail to see —"

"That'll be all," Riker snapped, still glaring at Magdalys. She stared right back at him, for once grateful that Von Marsh insisted on calling her the wrong name.

Riker finally turned away. "You may continue on your journey. Enjoy the theater." He slid off the wagon with that same fluid grace and signaled the still-spooked knuckleskull to fall back. And then Marietta gave the reins a tug and yelled "Heeyah!" and they were on their way. Magdalys glanced at the frightened faces of her friends, then looked up to the back of the wagon, where the magistrate stood staring at her with his searchlight eyes.

CHAPTER FOUR

A LETTER FROM THE FRONT

HENRIETTA VON MARSH still had the gram. She had the gram and she was holding it hostage in her ridiculous little purse.

Magdalys seethed. Around her, the theater crowd guffawed and cackled as three microraptors that had been adorned with flowers and fruits cavorted in ridiculous circles across the stage. In their midst, Halsey Crunk stood with his arms outstretched, makeup glistening with sweat, face scrunched into a mask of despair. He wore fake fangs, and two cardboard horns poked out of slicked-down hair. Just twenty years old, the young thespian had already made a worldwide name for himself. The black newspapers said he was the next James Hewlett or Ira Aldridge; white newspapers mocked him for doing

Shakespeare "in a Negro styling," but that just made him more infamous and in demand.

"Prospero does nap in the afternoon time, and then ye can brain him!"

"Ay, brain him!" someone shouted from the crowd. The room erupted with laughter again.

Halsey continued undaunted. "After stealing his magic books! Or perhaps you may drag your dagger across his throat."

Henrietta Von Marsh stood a few people over and back from Magdalys, looking very pale and uncomfortable in the sweaty crowd. She clutched her purse tightly against her chest and seemed to be holding her breath.

"Remember first to possess his books, for without them he's but a sot!" Halsey Crunk declared from the stage.

Magdalys had spent the first twenty minutes of the play trying to get rid of the creepy sensation that Magistrate Riker was still glaring at her from somewhere in the shadows. The only thing that distracted her was the rising frustration that someone had tried to reach her via gram and she had no idea what the message was. If she could get that purse away from Von Marsh, there was no way the matron would be able to follow her through the masses of people. Magdalys inched closer, trying not to look too obvious.

Cymbeline Crunk spun on stage in a swirly dress with butterfly wings strapped to her back; the colorful microraptors squawked and darted out of her way. "Ahh!" Cymbeline announced. "This plot I will tell my master, Prospero." The audience hissed at her character, Ariel's, treachery. Cymbeline was two years younger than her brother, and Magdalys thought she was the most beautiful person in the whole world. Her dark skin always seemed to glow in the stage lights like it was streaked with stardust, and she wore her thick hair in two magnificent globes on either side of her head.

Magdalys peeled her eyes away from the stage and squeezed through the crowd toward Von Marsh. Amaya stood in front of her beside Little Sabeen, both of them enraptured by the ruckus on stage. Mapper was nearby, hunched over some scrap of paper and fiddling with his glasses, ignoring the play entirely.

But where was Two Step?

Magdalys squinted around the dim theater. The room was full of black and brown folks from all over New York. Men and women and kids crowded up against each other, gazing through the smoky auditorium, their faces full of wonder and laughter. Something moved in the darkness of the rafters above. Magdalys squinted, then growled.

Two Step.

He clung to a wooden support beam, his legs dangling, looking down at the stage, smiling like a goofy madman. Magdalys shook her head. Marietta was busy taking care of Old Brimworth, who sat nodding her ancient wrinkly head as if she had a clue what was going on.

With a snarl, Halsey swung at Cymbeline, who dodged

daintily out of the way as the audience erupted into cheers and laughter. *Now!* Magdalys thought, reaching up and snatching Von Marsh's purse out of her hands and then shoving into the crowd.

Someone was going to have to be the adult in the situation, since the matrons were all too busy worrying about each other. Magdalys would stash her letter and go get Two Step down from the rafters, and then —

"MARGARET ROCHEFORD!" Henrietta Von Marsh's bark cut through Cymbeline Crunk's lovetorn speech. A hush swept across the whole auditorium as all eyes turned to the tall, elderly white woman in the middle of the room. Magdalys felt her face get hot. Von Marsh stood with her arms crossed over her chest. "Come back here this instant, young lady."

"Ay, stow your wid, lady!" someone yelled. The crowd jeered and jostled as the matron launched into it after Magdalys.

"You are three men of sin, whom destiny has belched up 'pon this island," Cymbeline crowed, rolling her eyes at the disturbance.

Seething, Magdalys ducked down and ran. Up above, Two Step let out a snicker.

Back by the entranceway, a little shaft of light cut through the shadowy theater. Magdalys made her way toward it, pulling the envelope from Von Marsh's purse and cradling it like a newborn baby against her chest.

"'Scuse me, pardon me, 'scuse me," she said, shoving her way through the crowd. Folks were too caught up in the play to really mind.

"My high charms work," Halsey, now playing Prospero and wearing a long white beard, declared on the stage. "And these, mine enemies, are all knit up in their distractions." One of the flower-adorned microraptors took that moment to let out an elongated fart, which sent the crowd into an explosion of laughter.

Magdalys positioned herself in front of the light shaft and pulled out the letter, willing her shaking hands to be still.

Dear Miss Magdalys Roca,

You don't know me, but my name is Pvt. Tennessee Summers. I am dictating this letter to Doc Billings, as I myself am illiterate, but I trust he will convey my words to you adequately. I serve alongside your brother in the African Brigade of the 9th Louisiana Regiment, Mounted Ceratops Division.

Mounted Ceratops Division? Montez didn't care much for dinos, and he'd definitely never ridden a trike. But . . . had he been killed? Her eyes welled up with tears at the thought, but she read on.

Your brother and I were defending a Union supply area at Milliken's Bend as part of General Grant's siege of the nearby city of Vicksburg. A regiment of Reb raptor riders assaulted our post and your brother was struck in the head by a rifle butt.

A rifle butt? That meant the fighting must've been fierce — hand-to-hand combat.

Magdalys tried to blink the tears away but they kept coming. Around her, the crowd and their laughter seemed suddenly very far away.

He's still alive, but he was wounded badly, and when I last left him in the medical tent, he was still unconscious.

She let out a breath she hadn't realized she'd been holding. At least he was alive. Or had been when the letter was written — she checked the date — three weeks earlier.

I am sorry to deliver such difficult news, as I know you are far away and still very young yourself, and so can do little. Your brother fought with incredible bravery. I myself was injured as well, though not as gravely, and we are going to be transported to New Orleans where we will be treated. I will do my very best to update whenever I possibly can, and pray this letter finds you safely.

Most Sincerely,
Private T. Summers
African Brigade
9th Louisiana Regiment
Mounted Ceratops Division

Magdalys lowered the letter and wiped her eyes. She placed it carefully inside the envelope and tucked the envelope inside her satchel. Slowly, the information seeped into her mind and became truth. Her brother had been assigned to a dinoriding division of the U.S. Army. He'd been ambushed — that alone was hard enough to wrap her head around. He was wounded, but he wasn't dead. Not yet. He was . . . alive.

He needed her.

She closed her eyes and took a deep, ragged breath.

Montez needed her and she was a million miles away.

But really, what could she do anyway? She wasn't a nurse, although she'd gotten more than enough experience helping the matrons tape up the other kids' scrapes and bruises. But she was the only family Montez had. And now he was alone and wounded, dying maybe, and . . . she had to get to him. Somehow.

Someone in the audience screamed, pulling Magdalys from her thoughts. It wasn't a stage scream; someone was truly terrified. Then more screams filled the air, which suddenly seemed very thick.

"Fire!" someone yelled, just as the crisp smell of ash and burning wood reached Magdalys's nose.

"FIRE!" the whole world seemed to scream at once, a sudden, deafening roar of terror. Up on stage, the actors stood frozen, staring at a flickering light that emanated from a far corner of the theater as the feathered microraptors shrieked and scattered.

The kids, Magdalys thought. *They'll be trampled. Or burned alive.* With a roar, the trickle of fleeing theatergoers suddenly became a stampede. An impenetrable, tangled mass swept toward Magdalys, flushed around her, and nearly toppled her as she stumbled along with them and out into the muggy Manhattan night.

CHAPTER FIVE
FIRE AT THE ZANZIBAR

MAGDALYS SCANNED THE fleeing crowd for her friends. Amaya would look out for Little Sabeen. And Mapper would stick by them; all three were probably ducking between people's legs toward the exit. Two Step, though . . . he could end up anywhere. What if he was trapped in the rafters?

Magdalys blinked through the billowing smoke, trying to make out the rooftop of the theater. Around her, people yelled and cried, still flooding out of the front doors. She heard the sound of glass exploding and ducked as flames burst out and flickered toward the dark sky. She glanced up and down the block — the rest of the Raptor Claw was quiet. A few dark figures darted along ramshackle storefronts and dilapidated tenements; theatergoers fled down darkened alleys. As usual, the Claw reeked of dino droppings and rotten lettuce.

There was no sign of any of the orphans.

Where were they?

Another burst of flame exploded from the theater, shattering more windows. They couldn't still be inside, they'd be . . . Magdalys shook away the thought, her teeth chattering in the cool night breeze. Maybe there was a back exit. They were all close by the stage. Surely the actors knew of another door — what if the orphans followed them out that way?

Magdalys pushed through the crowd, ignoring the tears and screams, and slipped down an alleyway alongside the theater. Tiny microsaurs scattered in the shadows, tittering with alarm as she passed. The low, mournful hooting of sauropods sounded across the city as Magdalys rounded the corner. There, in an open plaza behind the theater, Old Mother Virginia Brimworth leaned over, hacking up phlegmy balls of soot as Henrietta Von Marsh tended to her. Marietta Gilbert Smack and Cymbeline and Halsey Crunk ushered the orphans and a few other stragglers out of the smoky doorway. Up above, microdactyls flitted across the sky. *They would be carrying updates to the authorities*, Magdalys thought as she ran toward the matrons. The city-wide alarm had already sounded. The ground rumbled with the weight of oncoming sauropods. The fire brigades would arrive and everything would be alright.

Amaya and Little Sabeen stood beside each other. Smoke smudges dotted their brown faces and they both looked rattled but otherwise okay.

"Magdalys!" Amaya yelled as she ran up to them. They

embraced, and then Amaya pulled away to cough and Sabeen jumped up into Magdalys's arms and pressed herself against her face.

"The others?" Magdalys said.

"Here comes Mapper now," Marietta reported.

A squabble of costumed microraptors burst out of the doorway first, followed by Mapper, his glasses all smoked over and his dark skin smudged with ashes. Marietta herded him toward the others. "Where's Varney?" she yelled over the smashing windows and screams around them.

Everyone looked around. No Varney, no wagon in sight.

"Where did you leave him?" Von Marsh demanded.

"Right here! Is Mother Brimworth alright?" Marietta called.

Von Marsh shook her head, patting the older woman's back. "She seems to have inhaled quite a bit of smoke, I'm afraid."

"Where's Two Step?" Magdalys asked. "Last time I saw him he was —"

"There!" Mapper pointed up at the rooftop, where a small shadowy form appeared through the billowing smoke.

"We gotta get to him!" Magdalys cried.

"We could maybe get up from one of the other buildings," Cymbeline Crunk said. "Pass a ladder across the alleyway somehow." She was covered in soot and her dress was charred at the edges, but at least she seemed more or less together. Her brother, Halsey, on the other hand, had shuffled off into the shadows and was sobbing as the sparkling ashes of his life's work swirled around him.

"Where's the blistering fire brigade?" Von Marsh yelled. "They'd have a brachy, I'm sure, and they could get him." Flames blasted out from a back window and a series of cracks erupted from inside the theater.

"The foundations," Halsey Crunk whimpered. "The whole place'll go soon." He shook his head.

Magdalys looked around desperately. Something caught her eye down a street at the far end of the plaza — it was lit up. Not like streetlamps; a warmer, fuller glow, not unlike . . . the fire at the theater. She glanced at the sky, where a long dark plume of smoke rose above the rooftops and long graceful necks of sauropods.

"Something else . . ." Magdalys said. "Something else . . ."

"What?" Amaya asked.

People were running through the plaza now, dark figures bolting out of the alleyways, some mounted on clumsy, staggering knuckleskulls. The sound of breaking glass seemed to come from all around them, and then desperate cries for help.

"What's happening?" Little Sabeen moaned.

"It's an attack," Magdalys said.

"Who?" asked Mapper. "Who's attacking?"

"The draft offices started drawing names out of a tumbler today," Cymbeline said. "White folks are being conscripted for the war against the slaver states and they don't want to go.

There was word there could be some backlash against black New Yorkers, but this . . ." She shook her head.

That's why the city was so quiet, Magdalys thought. *Like it was holding its breath, waiting for . . . this.* She looked at the carnage around her. And this was only the beginning. *Riker knew this was going to happen, and he let us walk right into it . . .*

"We have to get your friend down before the structure gives out. And then we have to get out of here."

"The structure," Halsey muttered. "Gone. All of it. Ashes."

A policeman rode into the square, his knuckleskull stumbling in an awkward, rhythmless gait. The officer kept looking behind him, then up at the sky.

"We're saved!" Von Marsh squealed, waving at him as he approached. "Officer Swolt! Over here!"

"You must clear the square," Officer Swolt said, slowing his steed to an unsteady halt. "There's a disturbance in the Claw, I'm afraid. All civilians must clear out. Full curfew in effect." He readied to leave, apparently oblivious to the inferno that had once been a theater crackling just a few feet away.

"Wait!" Magdalys yelled. "We need help! Our friend is on the roof!"

Von Marsh pushed past her. "And Mother Brimworth has inhaled a terrible amount of smoke, Officer! She's already quite frail and needs medical treatment immediately!"

"Oh dear," Swolt said, steadying his mount again. He looked around, then his eyes seemed to finally settle on the ancient woman leaning on her cane in front of him. She let out a wheeze. "Oh dear," he said again. "Come on, then, up you go." He reached out a hand to Old Brimworth and, with Von Marsh pushing her from behind, hoisted her up into the knuckleskull's leather saddle. "We'll get you to the hospital."

"I'll come too," Von Marsh declared, scrambling up awkwardly before the officer could say no. "Marietta! Make sure the children make it back safely to the Asylum!" The knuckleskull reared back, almost throwing the lot of them, squawked once, and then wobbled off. "I'll take care of Mother Brimworth! Not to worry!"

Magdalys let out a scream, launching after them, but the dinosteed had already galloped off into the night.

CHAPTER SIX
BRACHY

THE CRISP SMELL of fire took over the world. Pops and crackles snarled from the wrecked theater. Off to the side, the Crunks and Marietta tried to corral all the children away from the flames. Magdalys could still see Two Step waving frantically from the roof, but the smoke kept getting thicker.

"Mags!" Little Sabeen yelled. "Come! We have to —"

Whatever she was going to say next was lost beneath the sudden rumbling that erupted all around them. *A brachy,* Magdalys thought. *The fire brigade . . .*

Sure enough, a long thick neck soon appeared over the rooftop as the thundering footsteps grew louder, and then the whole gigantic beast lumbered around a corner. It sent up a triumphant hoot as it skidded to a halt and a team of burly fellows with ash-stained faces leapt off. Two huge washbasins had been slung across the brachy's back, and the fire brigade went to work filling up buckets and rushing around with them.

"Hello?" Magdalys yelled. "My friend is on the roof! He's trapped!" But no one paid her any mind. "Can you guys just —"

Magdalys froze. The distinct feeling that someone was staring at her crept up her spine and settled into her brain. She looked up, followed the long, graceful curve of that neck as it arched into the firelit sky, and found herself gaping directly into the huge, sleepy eye of the brachy. And was it . . . was it smiling?

Arruumph!! The sound seemed to burst from inside of her, and Magdalys took a step back, her mouth open.

Um . . . she thought. *Hello?*

The brachy threw its big head back and trumpeted into the night.

"Quiet, you!" one of the firemen yelled. "We don't need the damn Rusty Raptors getting territorial now, do we?"

She'd managed to convince herself what happened with Varney might've somehow been a coincidence, but this . . . ? It hooted again as if to confirm Magdalys's thought.

"Quiet, I said!" The fireman directed a sharp kick at the dinosaur's leg.

"Incoming!" another one hollered, just as a growl came from the opposite end of the plaza.

"Oh, now you've done it!" the first one spat.

A purple-and-brown raptor stepped out in front of the

burning theater. It was emaciated and bedraggled, with a few shredded orange feathers along its arms. Its foot claw was missing on one side and an eye on the other, which somehow made the thing all the more horrifying. On its back, a grim-looking mustached man in a cowboy hat brandished an old-fashioned blunderbuss, its wide metal mouth extending back over a wooden handle. Two more raptors stepped out behind it, both with armed riders on top. Their big yellow eyes surveyed the fire brigade, squinting and widening again. They swooped those long necks low, glancing back and forth, and then rose back up to their full, terrifying height.

"The Raptor Claw is Double R territory," the lead rider said. "Maybe you haven't seen the updated maps."

Magdalys saw Sabeen and Amaya duck into the shadows, hopefully with the others.

"And we're here to save this building," one of the fire brigadiers said. "So you're welcome. Now kindly move out of our way so we can do our jobs."

The raptor rider released a surly smile. "That's not how this works. We didn't authorize anyone to put out any fires."

The firemen exchanged uneasy glances. The oldest of them, the same one who'd kicked the brachy, took a step forward. "There are more of us than there are of them, lads," he said, chest puffed out. "Let's take 'em." The brigade drew billy clubs and axes and let out a single, unified "Huzzah!" before rushing forward.

Magdalys held back a scream of frustration. None of this

was helping! Two Step was still on the roof and the theater was still burning, and . . .

Arrrrooooooooorrrrrrghhh!!

The sound came from inside her again, and this time it was an irritated growl that so matched her own frustration she thought she herself might've made it. But then she looked up at the towering beast and found it glaring at the unfolding carnage. A raptor had already grabbed one of the firemen in its maw and hurled him across the plaza. Three more had been knocked over by a tail swipe, and the leader was swinging his billy club uselessly at the tallest raptor.

The brachy looked back down at Magdalys and another frustrated call erupted through her. *Maybe,* Magdalys thought, taking a step toward the brachy. *Just maybe.* She reached out a trembling hand, took another step forward. Her hand landed on the thick hide. It was warm and glistened in the firelight. It felt rough like a tree trunk, but seemed to pulse with all that wild reptilian life.

The brachy is very stubborn but very loyal, Dr. Barlow Sloan wrote in the Dinoguide. *Once the brachy has been properly trained and domesticated, it will follow its rider into the most intolerable situations. But if it senses uncertainty or deception, it will be near impossible to get it to do anything.*

Magdalys narrowed her eyes. *Fine, then,* she thought. *No deception here. No uncertainty.* She needed this brachy to help Two Step and get everyone out of there, since no one else would do it. She made her way along its flank to where a rope ladder hung down from the worn leather saddle beside one of the water basins. Without giving time for another doubt to creep in, she grabbed the ladder and scurried up it.

This was real. She was about to ride a dino. Or try anyway. As terrifying as the world had suddenly become, a tiny part of Magdalys thrilled at the touch of the brachy's hide, the sting of the rope ladder in her hands, the way this huge, magnificent creature encompassed the whole world when she was this close to it, even the dank reek of it filling her nostrils.

Raptor snarls and the shouts of wounded men still rose from the plaza. She heaved herself up to the saddle and swung her leg over the side. Before she could even find her balance, the brachy hooted once and then lunged forward, reaching the burning theater in three massive clomps.

"Whoa!" Magdalys yelled, almost sliding right out of the saddle and into the middle of the plaza. Undaunted by the flames (it was a fire brigade dino, after all), the brachy craned its long neck to the edge of the rooftop, where Two Step stood with his mouth hanging open.

"Jump!" Magdalys yelled.

"Oy!" one of the firemen called. "That's our brachy! What the devil?"

Two Step just stood there panting for a few seconds.

"Two Step!" Magdalys yelled. "Come! On!"

He leapt, arms outstretched, and landed belly-first on the dino's snout. The brachy tipped its head back toward the sky and sent Two Step sliding face-first down its neck, toward Magdalys.

"AAAAAAAAH!!" Two Step yelled as he careened into her and they both tumbled backward in the saddle.

"You climb every! Single! Thing!" Magdalys yelled, standing up and dusting herself off. "And then you have to do this *one* thing to save your own life and you freeze up! Jeez, man!"

"I'm sorry!" Two Step stammered, but then they both fell back down as the brachy reared back, letting out a terrified howl. "Um . . . Magdalys . . . I think we're in trouble."

Two of the raptors screeched and hurled into the air toward them.

CHAPTER SEVEN
KA-BLAM!

KA-BLAM!!

Both raptors shrieked and landed suddenly, their heads cowed; a low, rattling growl filled the air as they glanced back and forth.

Magdalys realized she'd ducked without meaning to. The brachy had landed his front two legs and then sidestepped uneasily at the blast, the great neck craning around to see where it had come from. The shot had sounded like it came from everywhere at once, but most of all somewhere behind Magdalys and off to the side.

"What the—?" one of the riders started, and then Magdalys saw Cymbeline Crunk step forward, still in full costume, fairy wings and all, with a double-barreled shotgun raised. And then the world seemed to explode again as she blasted a second shot over everyone's heads. The raptors backstepped so quickly, one rider fell headlong onto the cobblestones and then scrambled up and bolted.

"Let's go," Cymbeline said, grabbing one of the leather straps on the brachy's saddle and dangling herself alongside the huge dino, shotty pointed forward. "We gotta get the others."

Magdalys and Two Step traded a wide-eyed gape, and then Magdalys turned back to the brachy. "Come on, big fella," she whispered.

"Um, did you just talk to the dino?" Two Step asked.

With a harrumphing sound that Magdalys wasn't sure if everyone could hear or just her, the brachy strode into the crowd of stunned tusslers.

"And did it *listen* to you?" Two Step said.

"Mind ya business," Magdalys snorted.

"This is Rusty Rapt —" one of the riders started.

"Ah, shut it, hickjop," Cymbeline ordered. The Rusty Raptors all clammed up accordingly, eyes wide. "My smoothbore will blast a hole or twelve in each of you while you're still fiddling with the ramrod of your grandma's blunderbuss there." There was a pause, and the riders looked back and forth at each other uneasily. "Now scatter, you moose-face loobies." The Rusty Raptors didn't have to be told twice. She was right, after all, and anyway her tone left no room for discussion.

"I think I'm in love," Two Step said.

Magdalys rolled her eyes. "She's out of your league, bro." She squinted into the shadows. "Everyone climb on! We gotta get back to the Asylum."

Mapper dashed out into the open, followed by Amaya and Little Sabeen. Finally Halsey Crunk stumbled out too, his tears tracking tiny rivers through the soot on his face, and then Marietta Gilbert Smack, the hem of her long elegant skirts coated in the grime of the Raptor Claw.

"Which way?" Magdalys asked.

Once everyone had piled on, the brachy had stomped out of the plaza and into the darkened streets of Manhattan. The yells of fighting and sharp crackle of smashing glass blended with dinosaur growls and occasional musket shots in a rising tide of terror that seemed to seep from the streets all around them.

Now they stood by the black waters of the Hudson River, gazing out at the few scattered lights of New Jersey.

"North," Mapper reported from behind Magdalys.

"Duh," Magdalys snapped back. "Which way is north?"

"Right!" Cymbeline and Mapper said at the same time.

"Got it." Magdalys put her face against the brachy's big warm neck and thought about the route along the river up to Forty-Second Street, then Fifth Avenue where the orphanage was. Safety, or the closest thing to it anyway. The brachy swung right and lumbered forward.

The Colored Orphan Asylum had never really felt like home to Magdalys. Those long cold hallways echoed with footsteps and sobs; the matrons, their faces usually tight, mouths full of reprimands and clunkily adjusted names. The only friendly face besides the other kids' was old Mr. Calloway's. He'd slip Magdalys and the others candies sometimes, and they heard him humming to himself to the swish of his broom and squeak of his well-shined boots as they fell asleep.

A shot rang out, not far away. Everyone huddled close and the brachy picked up his pace a little. Cymbeline loaded a few more shells into her shotgun and drew a long breath. Magdalys scanned the dimly lit shacks on the far side of the street. Nothing stirred.

In the distance, a few sauropods loomed over the rooftops of those huge dinofeed storehouses, long, graceful silhouettes against the cloudy night. Surely the National Guard would be deployed, with riots this bad. But most of them were probably down in Pennsylvania, where the Confederates were said to be making a desperate stab into Union territory, marauding through the farmlands and capturing free blacks to send south to slavery.

And somewhere down there, Montez lay in a hospital bed, or maybe on some dirty floor, unconscious and wounded. Magdalys shuddered. Who would care for him? Who would keep him safe? Certainly not the same army that had already hurled him into harm's way. Rumors swirled about Union generals sending the colored units out to be massacred with inefficient gear and less pay than the white soldiers. Magdalys had to find out if he was okay. Except she'd never know for sure, not really. Montez was the only family she had left in this country, and he needed her. Or, if she was being honest, she needed him. Maybe, somehow, she could . . .

CRACK!!

The gunshot was much closer this time, only a block away. Another one rang out, even closer, and then the shriek of a raptor. Magdalys could just glimpse figures moving through the darkness. Were they coming toward where the brachy strode along beside the river? She couldn't tell.

A small, roundish shape scattered along the ground nearby. Then another. Magdalys squinted through the darkness. A herd of tiny microceratopses scuttled past, squealing and grunting. The little guys were like baby, hornless trikes. *They served no discernible purpose in society,* Dr. Barlow Sloan insisted somewhat caustically in the Dinoguide, *except to get in the way and occasionally be household pets.* The brachiosaurus paused to watch them hurry off and hooted sympathetically.

"Uh, Mag-D?" Two Step whispered. "Since you seem to be able to wrangle this brachy pretty well, could you tell her to, like . . . hurry?"

"He."

"What?"

"The brachy's a he, not a she. And . . . yes."

Magdalys didn't even close her eyes or concentrate too hard this time. She just thought *Go!* and then they were blasting along beside the Hudson at a breakneck gallop, and the wild night wind rushed through her hair and for a few flickering seconds she felt like everything might somehow be alright.

CHAPTER EIGHT
A REFUGE IN RUINS

THE SMELL OF charred wood and smoke met them as they turned away from the river, and Magdalys's heart sank. She'd seen the dark plume rising into the sky as they'd gotten close, had held out hope it was some other building, maybe . . . maybe . . .

She guided the huge dinosaur up Fifth Avenue toward the still-smoldering wreckage of the Colored Orphan Asylum. Groups of revelers or rioters, or whatever they were, wandered in the opposite direction, looking for more trouble to get into. They seemed to be having a lovely time. Did no one care that someone's home was up in flames?

"No," Magdalys whispered as they entered the open area where the orphanage once stood. "No!" It came out as a scratchy yell. Behind her, she heard the gasps and moans of her friends. Where were the rest of the orphans? Had they . . . had they died?

"What have they done?" Marietta screamed.

One by one, they slid off the brachy and stumbled forward through the debris-filled street. The orphanage was the last bit of twine tethering her to New York City, and now it was gone. A tiny gear turned in Magdalys's heart, the only ray of light she could find in this terrible night: She would head south as soon as she could, find Montez. She would find Montez, in New Orleans maybe, or wherever he was along the way, and stay by his side until he woke up. She'd learn to be a nurse if that's what it took to stay with him. The U.S. Army needed nurses, she was sure of it. Now all she needed was to find some way to get down there. And survive this night . . .

"No!" Two Step yelled, running ahead.

Magdalys took off after him. "Wait!" That boy was always in a hurry to get into the worst possible situation, she thought. Then she stopped dead in her tracks. Two Step had stopped too. They both stared up at the dark shape dangling from a lamppost in front of them.

Mr. Calloway.

She knew him from his shoes. Those old Union Army boots he wore; said his son had sent them from the front lines to make sure his ol' man had something sturdy on his feet. Magdalys could tell Mr. Calloway shined them every day. Even though they were beat-up and had probably been discarded by some soldier, Mr. Calloway managed to keep them looking spiffy somehow.

And now they were all that was left to be recognized of him.

A sorrow deeper than any Magdalys had ever felt before welled up inside her. It felt like the ocean was rising from her tummy, shoving its way through her chest, and trying to explode out of her face.

"How . . . could they . . ." Two Step stammered. "Mr. Calloway was . . ." He just shook his head. Magdalys understood. No words made any sense.

Behind them, Cymbeline shrieked and Little Sabeen burst into tears. Magdalys heard Amaya comfort her and then say, "Mapper, watch her. I'll be right back."

Be right back? Magdalys thought. *Where —*

And then Amaya strode past her, past Mr. Calloway, and directly into the smoldering ruins of the orphanage.

Sparkling ash and black flakes of debris spun through the air around Magdalys as she jumped over burnt logs and ducked through the half-collapsed entranceway after Amaya.

Mr. Calloway's body still dangled in the front of her mind; it felt like someone had put the image on a hot iron and branded it across her forehead. She would never forget. But right now she had to stay alive; that was the most important thing. Later, she would mourn, let it all come flowing out, sob and sob and sob, but not yet. Otherwise . . .

Something cracked above them. "Amaya!" Magdalys screamed as a flaming chunk of plaster plummeted from the rafters. Amaya looked up and leapt out of the way, landing with an impressive forward roll and springing back up. "How did you . . . ?" Magdalys stuttered. In all the years she'd known Amaya, she'd never seen her move like that. Amaya just smirked sourly and turned back to the hallway she'd been heading toward.

Magdalys hurried after. "Amaya! Where are you going? At least let me . . . let me help you?" She finally caught up and fastwalked alongside her through the dark corridor.

The flames hadn't done nearly as much damage to the back half of the Colored Orphan Asylum. The whole area was coated in black soot and it looked like a pack of feral ceratopses had barged through, but at least the walls were still standing.

"The files," Amaya said in a quiet voice clenched with rage. "*Our* files."

"Amaya, we could all die, like, at any moment! Don't you get that? Even if we make it out of here alive, the mob that did this could come back and —"

Amaya stopped, turned her sad face to Magdalys. "Our stories are our lives, Mag. Even if they're incomplete and written by strangers. They're all we've got of who we are, where we come from." She turned and briskly walked around a corner.

Magdalys followed, found Amaya standing before a shattered doorway. The records room. The orphans weren't even allowed near this place, as signs all around the hallway insisted in red, menacing letters. "You with me?" Amaya asked.

Magdalys nodded once and then kicked away the battered remnants of the door. They strode in side by side.

CHAPTER NINE
THE RECORDS ROOM

THE HEFTY LEDGER books waited on a huge wooden bookshelf that took up the far wall of the dim room. How many broken lives and secrets did that monster hold in its bowels, Magdalys wondered as they stepped up to it. "Okay, look," Amaya said. "It's sorted in alphabetical order, not year, so . . ."

"We have to find —"

"Each of our files."

"You get yours, plus Two Step and Sabeen's. I'll find mine and Mapper's."

They got to work. Outside, the city still convulsed with rioting and looting. She hoped the others were safe, but she had to put all that out of her head and concentrate on the scribbled names flying beneath her fingers. So many children . . . There'd been no sign of anyone around, which probably meant they all got away before the fire got them. Mr. Calloway had probably been giving them time to escape, fending off the attackers when . . .

She tried to shake away the thought, refocus on the names. *Raymond, June. Richmond, Alfred. Roaner, Mary.* All these names, each belonging to a young person, a young person who might be lying dead somewhere right now, or worse . . . "Aha!" Magdalys yelled when she saw her own name. She tore the pages right out of the book, along with those of Montez, Julissa, and Celia. Amaya gave her a quick nod of approval and went back to leafing through the ledger she'd pulled. A sound came from the corridor, then another. Footsteps. Magdalys and Amaya both leapt to their feet at the same time.

"Girls!" Cymbeline yelled, rounding the corner, shotgun at the ready. Marietta was behind her, looking up and down the hallway, wielding a charred table leg in both hands like a bat. "What on earth are you doing?"

Amaya lowered a metal paperweight she'd had poised to hurl. Magdalys exhaled, realizing just how trapped and exposed they had been. And distracted to boot. Aaand in the burnt remains of a torched orphanage.

"We're getting our files," Amaya said, as if that was the most obvious thing in the world. "You can either help us or you can leave."

"But —" Marietta started, her eyes wide.

“Fast then,” Cymbeline said, cutting her off. “Which ones do you already have?”

“Magdalys has hers and I’m getting mine. She’s got Two Step, so Cymbeline, take Sabeen’s — her last name’s Clark — and Marietta, find Mapper — his real name’s Kyle. Last name’s —”

“Tannery,” Marietta said, crossing the room. “I know.”

Cymbeline was already pulling open a ledger. For a few minutes, they searched in silence. Then, one by one, they each let out little yelps of victory and ripped pages free. “Come on,” Cymbeline said. “We left the rest with Halsey and . . . he’s not well.” They hurried back through the ruins, made it back out into the thick night air, files in hand, and started across the lawn.

“Come on,” Two Step yelled. “They’re coming back!”

Magdalys’s tummy lurched as she saw Mr. Calloway’s body still dangling from the lamppost. Beyond that, Mapper was scrambling back onto the brachy while Halsey Crunk pointed an old flintlock pistol at something Magdalys couldn’t see. Two Step ran up to them as they passed beneath Mr. Calloway’s boots. “Another dinogang showed up,” Two Step explained. “Mr. Crunk took some shots at ’em and they ran off but we seen ’em scurrying around the shadows again just over there!”

“Back!” Halsey yelled. He cocked the pistol with a loud click as Two Step, then Marietta clamored up the side of the brachy. Halsey let the hammer fall; a *fizzzz* sounded, and with a smoky blast, the pistol fired. Magdalys flinched at the bang, then grabbed hold of the stirrup and scrabbled up. The brachy took an uneasy step forward. *Easy,* Magdalys whispered in her mind. *Eeeasy.*

"Go," Cymbeline ordered, patting her brother on the shoulder. "Everyone get on." She popped some more shells in the chamber of her shotgun. Halsey climbed halfway up; Magdalys and Two Step reached down and grabbed his sweaty hands, pulled him the rest of the way. Amaya was still catching up behind him.

"Which way?" Magdalys asked Mapper.

"Depends. Where we going?"

Magdalys glanced out into the street, where a few scattered figures seemed to dance amidst the shadows. A handful of blocks north lay the huge wilderness that an early black settlement had been cleared out of to make room for the Dumping Grounds. Stegosaurs would haul massive carts full of collected dinopoop up there at the end of each day: you could catch whiffs of it all the way downtown. There were rumored to be vicious feral raptorpacks lurking amidst the stink piles, and possibly even a wild tyrannosaurus or two. So that was out.

On the other side, smoke still rose in thick plumes over the rooftops as the riots raged on. The Dinofeed Warehouse District might've offered them somewhere to hide, but they'd already passed it, and clearly the rioters were running around there too. And the Raptor Claw seemed to be the very heart of so much of the rioting. The Stinkpit, a rugged sprawl of collapsing tenement buildings adjacent to the Claw, probably wasn't any safer. She shook her head. "I don't know. Seems like there's nowhere safe for us."

"Head south and east toward the river," Cymbeline said. "I have an idea."

The brachy took another step forward, anxious to bolt. *Hold, big fella,* Magdalys thought. *Almost time.* Then a raptor emerged a few blocks away, its shiny, bloodred body bent forward in a low stalking position, the hooded rider leaning all the way back to stay balanced. The dino began slinking along Fifth Avenue, snout close to the ground. The rider raised something to his mouth, a whistle, Magdalys realized, just as the shrill blast rang out. The brachy stumbled forward a few startled steps.

"Come on!" Magdalys yelled.

Amaya was halfway up the saddle, holding the satchel of files out for them with one hand. Two Step snatched them, passed them to Mapper, and then helped her the rest of the way up. Cymbeline jogged along beside them, steadying her shotgun, and then just shook her head and swung herself alongside the saddle.

Behind them, three, no, four ankylosaurs skittered out onto the street ahead of the raptor. Thick horns curved like an elaborate headdress around their lumpy faces and rows of short spikes ran across their sand-colored bodies. Dr. Barlow Sloan described ankylosaurs as *irritable but reliable steeds, excellent for skirmishes or short-distance travel, less so for sustained battle or overnight trips.* Hooded riders sat astride each of those armored backs. They brandished whips and clubs, and they were galloping straight for the brachy.

Go! Magdalys commanded. *Go!*

Magdalys saw a flash from somewhere behind them and a musket shot cracked across the night, dinging a lamppost they were passing. The brachy swerved wildly, nearly throwing them all over the side.

They'd left Mr. Calloway, Magdalys realized, tightening her grip on the saddle. Left him hanging there, all alone and dead and never to sing them to sleep again. She shook her head, tears welling up.

Ka-blam! Another musket shot rang out and Magdalys looked back. She caught a glint of light off the circular medallion on the rider's robes just as he reached up and lowered his hood. Magistrate Riker's smiling face glared back at her. The brachy let out a howl and broke into a frantic dash.

CHAPTER TEN
RUN!

GA-GUNG! GA-GUNG! GA-GUNG! They charged down Fifth Avenue, the whole world a series of shuddering earthquakes, the dark, burning city a blur around them. Magdalys saw a stream of blood trickle from the brachy's flank. *No!* The poor guy. He had already saved their lives and now he'd been wounded. Shot! She could tell he was favoring the opposite side as they thundered along.

Stay calm, big guy, Magdalys cooed in her mind. The reply was only another desperate hoot blurted out into the night.

"Know how to shoot an old flintlock?" Cymbeline asked, sliding up alongside Magdalys at the back of the saddle.

"Uh-uh," Magdalys said. She glanced back. The raptor had stayed at a slow stalk, presumably so Riker could get off a good shot, but the ankys scrambled forward at an unsettling speed. She saw one of the riders swing his whip over his head — and then fly backward when a metal bucket came tumbling through the sky and cracked him across the face.

"Got 'im!" Mapper yelled. Beside him, Two Step foraged through the saddlebags for more fire equipment they could use as projectiles.

"Here," Cymbeline said, handing Magdalys the flintlock pistol and a powder case. "Sorry my brother's so old-fashioned. I've been trying to get him to upgrade to a caplock for months. You're gonna have to learn fast. Hurled buckets aren't gonna stop ol' Rich Riker, I'm afraid."

"We bumped into him earlier," Magdalys said. "But he was with the cops, not these guys . . ."

Cymbeline cast a wary eye toward where Riker and his raptor lurked along through the shadows of Forty-First Street. "The Kidnapping Club. I'll explain later. For now, get one of those cartridges and pour some powder into the flashpan." She turned back to the attacking dinoriders, shotgun raised, while Magdalys scrambled in the bag, pulled out a little paper packet, and then held up the gun with trembling hands. The flashpan was the little chamber above the trigger that the hammer brought the flint down onto. She tore open the packet.

"Not too much powder," Cymbeline said without looking down. "You need most of it to pour down the muzzle."

Ka-BLAM!! Cymbeline's shotgun screamed, and Magdalys nearly dropped the bag of powder. A sharp ping sounded: the ball ricocheting off the armored back of one of those ankys.

"I can help," Amaya said, crouching beside Magdalys. On any other day, Magdalys would have been shocked by this, but after seeing how Amaya jumped away from that burning debris and was ready to clock Cymbeline when they surprised them in the records room . . . pieces were beginning to fall into place about this quiet girl with long black hair.

"Good." Cymbeline shuck-shucked the shell away and took aim again.

"Here." Amaya took the bag, poured a few grains of black powder into the flashpan, and then lowered the frizzen over it, keeping it safely packed away. "Pour the rest down the barrel."

Magdalys did as she was told, holding the edge of the packet against the mouth of the barrel so she wouldn't spill any while the brachy crashed along through the streets.

Ka-BLAM! Cymbeline's shotgun roared again. This time, a man's voice hollered in answer, and Magdalys heard the crash and tumble of a body falling onto the cobblestones. *Was he dead?* She stared down the dark street.

Ka-piiiing! A musket ball ricocheted off the armored plating around the brachy's saddle a few feet from them.

BLAM!! Cymbeline took one shot, then another, then shuck-shucked the shells out.

"Now the ball goes in," Amaya said, retrieving it herself and popping it into the muzzle. "And then the —"

"Ramrod," Magdalys said, pulling the slender metal shaft out from beneath the barrel and shoving it into the front of the pistol. "That part I know."

BLAM!! Cymbeline let off another shot. An anky squealed and veered into a lamppost, hurling its rider through the air. "There we go!" Cymbeline yelled. "Gotta aim for the face."

Magdalys cringed. She knew the dino's rider was directing it to attack her, but she couldn't help but feel for the poor beast anyway.

"Flint in place," Amaya said, wrestling a little black shard into the hammer. "And we're good to go." Magdalys stared at the loaded pistol in her hand for a second.

"Heads up," Two Step yelled. The last ankyrider had pulled alongside them; he swung a club with nails sticking out. Magdalys raised the pistol, her hand shaking, cocked it back, and pulled the trigger. The hammer fell and sparks danced out of the chamber with a *fizz!* Then it felt like her fingers were being shoved through a meat grinder as the gun let off an ear-shattering *BANG!* and smoke poured out. Magdalys stumbled backward into Amaya, who steadied her.

When the smoke cleared, the rider was still galloping along beside them. He'd lowered into his saddle, cringing, and now looked up, realized he hadn't been hit, and raised the spiked club again.

"I missed!" Magdalys said. A tiny part of her was relieved she hadn't killed someone; the rest screamed with terror that they were all about to die because of her bad shooting.

The rider brought his club down on the brachy's thick hide as a bucket flew past him and clanged onto the street. The brachy howled, swerving away, but the club stayed fast and the rider held tight, swinging off his mount. He scowled beneath a thick gray mustache, pulled a dagger from his belt, and shoved it into the brachy. Magdalys didn't have time to reload and Cymbeline was busy trading shots with Riker. She gripped the pistol by the muzzle and brought it down as hard as she could on the man's face.

"Garg!" he grunted, but his grip held tight. Then Magdalys flew backward and the city around them spun into a wild blur. The panicked brachy was turning. *No!* Magdalys thought, trying to steady herself. She saw the rider she'd just pistol-whipped fly off to the side and crash into a building wall, then slump beneath it and lie still. Cymbeline was already shoving her way to the front of the brachy's saddle as she loaded more shells into her double-barrel.

Sha-piiing! Another musket ball dinged off a streetlamp near them. The brachy reared to a halt and hooted his terror into the night. Mapper and Two Step were still helping each other up when Magdalys hurried past them to where Cymbeline was steadying her double-barrel for a shot. Up ahead, Riker's raptor had raised itself to full height. This one wasn't like the bedraggled old dino they'd squared up with outside the theater. This creature was almost twice the size and clearly well taken care of. Finely groomed purple and black feathers sprouted from its slender arms, and each razor-like claw on its feet had been shined and sharpened.

"Give up, Cymbeline," Rich Riker called. "As city magistrate, I demand you hand over the children to the custody of the State of New York."

"You mean the Kidnapping Club," Cymbeline spat.

Riker smiled. "In fact, you are technically the one kidnapping. These are wards of the state. Now that their home has oh so sadly been destroyed" — his smile widened — "it's up to the state to make sure they are properly cared for."

Riker's foul grin left no question in Magdalys's mind. He had been responsible for the Asylum burning down. He'd probably made sure Mr. Calloway was killed too. And he was surely after whatever other orphans had escaped, if he hadn't already snatched them up. And now he wanted custody of her and her friends? Rage seethed in her heart as she glared down Fifth Avenue. She felt Amaya stand beside her, knew that the others had stood now too, were behind them and wondering what would happen.

"You're not selling these kids into slavery," Cymbeline called. Then, under her breath: "I can't get a good shot off from this far away."

Magdalys handed Amaya the pistol, heard her start to prepare it. "Then we'll have to get closer," Magdalys said.

Cymbeline cocked an eyebrow. "Huh?"

"Get ready." Magdalys closed her eyes. Reached out for the brachy with her mind. *Forward,* she urged. *Run!* The brachy stirred beneath them. His worried trill sounded through Magdalys's mind. *I know you're scared,* she cooed. *So am I, believe me. But the only way we're gonna get out of this is by going all the way in. Now . . .* She felt the brachy's whole attention on her, its fear transforming into something different, hope maybe.

CHARGE! Magdalys thought with everything in her.

There was a pause and the city seemed to hold its breath. Then the brachy leapt forward, breaking into a full gallop without so much as a windup.

"Whoa!" Cymbeline yelled, raising her shotgun. In the street ahead, the raptor raised and lowered its clawed feet uneasily, and Riker lifted his rifle, eyes wide. "What are you — ?" But the brachy was already bearing down on him. He pulled tight on his reins, swinging the raptor off to the side, and then dug his stirrups hard, urging it into a pounce.

The raptor leapt just as the brachy charged past, and Cymbeline and Amaya were ready for it. Both their weapons blasted at the same time, one shot tearing into Riker's arm and the other sending the raptor sprawling backward with a shriek.

"Nice shot!" Cymbeline yelled. "Magdalys, whatever you're doing, keep doing it!"

In the dusty cloud behind them, Riker scrambled to his feet, clutching his wounded shoulder. His eyes met with Magdalys's as he pulled out a pistol and stood over the writhing raptor. He put the muzzle to its head.

A single shot rang out in the burning New York night as the brachy galloped away.

CHAPTER ELEVEN
THE RIVER CROSSING

"IT SHOULD BE here," Cymbeline said, sliding down from the saddle. It was the first time during this whole terrible night that Magdalys had heard her sound worried. "I guess the riots have thrown everything off. Still . . ." She squinted at the East River; the crescent moon above danced its broken light across the black ripples. Magdalys followed Cymbeline's gaze. Brooklyn was a dark mass on the other side, speckled with a few flickering lanterns along the shore. Further back, steeples rose above gaslit streets.

Safety, Magdalys thought. There were no riots or burning over there, not that she'd ever heard of. She could see it, but it was still so far away.

"We'll have to wait some," Cymbeline said. She turned

away from the water, her face tense. "I don't like it, but I don't know what else we can do. I'll take first watch." She loaded a few shells into her shotgun and cocked it ready, striding toward the small footpath through the shrubbery they'd come in from.

The brachy had carried them for almost an hour through the riot-torn streets of Manhattan. At first, Magdalys had just sent him along a random series of turns in case Riker or any of his Kidnapping Club tried to follow them. They'd passed a huge battalion of policemen, looking worn-out, some badly injured, but nightsticks drawn and clearly marching back into the fray. Pretty soon after that, Cymbeline started giving directions, guiding them gradually east and south toward the river.

And now it was time to part. The huge dinosaur couldn't cross the river with them — it would be too conspicuous to ride around Brooklyn — and there was no way to go back into that nightmare. Everyone dismounted, patting his massive flanks and thanking him before gathering around Cymbeline. Magdalys waited till they'd all gotten off and then gazed over at the brachy's battered hip. The gunshot looked pretty superficial, from what she could tell. The bleeding had stopped and the wound wasn't deep. A nasty bruise had blossomed around the scraped area where the ankyrider had tried to board them, but otherwise the fire brachy seemed to be okay. She rubbed his scaly skin lovingly. "You alright, big guy?"

Arrrreeooooommph, the brachy hooted. It sounded like it might've been a yes, Magdalys thought, trying to ignore the part of her that was still in total disbelief about talking to dinos.

"You need anything?"

The brachy leaned his massive neck forward into the darkness, and then Magdalys heard a splashing and gurgling from the river. He swung his big face back toward her a moment later and she jumped out of the way as a massive *splortch* of dinosaliva-tinged river water gushed over his wounded skin.

Ar-ar-ar-ar, the brachy's voice chortled inside Magdalys. He was laughing, she realized with a smile.

She slid down off the saddle, landing with a splish in a dark puddle, and wrapped herself around one of his great big tree trunk legs. "Thank you for saving our lives," she whispered.

The brachy hooted a loud song into the air and then rumbled off toward the city.

"This way," Cymbeline said as Magdalys joined the rest of them. Up ahead, there was a rickety old building by the water with a sign that said BREUKLYN FERRY PORT. "This is the old docking bay," Cymbeline explained. "It got replaced by a fancy one downtown, but we still use this sometimes to smuggle goods back and forth."

But there was no ferry to be found. Not even the telltale torches on the far shore to at least let them know it was on its way back.

A few battered old chairs formed a semicircle by the water, and Magdalys, Two Step, Sabeen, Mapper, and Amaya pulled them close to each other and huddled close. Marietta and

Halsey stood by the ferry port, talking quietly. It sounded like Halsey might be crying again, but Magdalys wasn't sure.

"Here," Amaya said, taking the files out of her satchel and passing them around. "Find yours."

A chorus of oohs and aahs rose as Mapper, Two Step, and Sabeen pulled open their folders. Magdalys held hers closed in her lap. She looked over at Amaya, who was doing the same.

A few moments passed while everyone read. "Whoa," Two Step said. "My parents. They were killed trying to escape a plantation. After they'd left me with someone to smuggle me up north."

"Wow . . ." Little Sabeen said. "I'm so sorry."

Two Step shook his head, wiped a tear away. "I had no idea. I mean I didn't think . . . they were alive, but . . . I don't know . . ." He wiped his eyes again but the tears kept falling around his red knuckles and down his cheeks.

Magdalys scootched next to him and put an arm around Two Step's shoulders. "I'm sorry, man."

"If it makes you feel any better," Mapper said, "actually, it probably won't. That was the wrong thing to say. Sorry, man."

"It really was," Amaya said.

"I said I was sorry!"

"It's fine," Two Step said. "I mean, it's not, but not because of what you said. I'm just happy I'm here with you guys and we're all still alive, even if . . . yeah. What's y'all's docs say?"

"Nothing, basically," Mapper said, holding up an almost blank sheet of paper. He shrugged. "But I knew that. Got rounded up from the streets and shoved in the Asylum by one of those creepy charity ladies. I never knew my parents. What about you, Sabeen?"

"I don't remember anything about mine either," Sabeen said. "This says my mom was a . . ." She squinted at the paper, read the words slowly: "Public woman. She died of yellow fever. And for my dad it just says *unknown*." She looked like she might cry, then seemed to gather herself, turned a firm gaze to the river.

"You're not gonna open yours, Amaya?" Magdalys asked quietly as the others talked more about their files.

She shook her head. "I already know what it says. I just needed it for legal reasons."

Magdalys wanted to ask her who on earth she was, this strange, slender girl who seemed to know everything from battle tactics to acrobatics, but she restrained herself. If Amaya wanted to tell her, she would. Clearly she'd kept her own secrets for this long, why would she start divulging now?

"What about you?" Amaya asked. She turned to Magdalys with a gentle smile on her face and suddenly seemed much older than everyone, even the Crunks and Marietta. Magdalys could count on one hand the number of times she'd seen Amaya smile. "Go head, open it."

She'd grabbed hers, Montez's, and Julissa's and Celia's, because one day she'd see them all again, she knew she would, and the files would be a welcome gift, a strange shard of memorabilia from this broken time, and maybe they'd all laugh about what they'd been through, all those years apart. Now her heart rattled into overdrive at the thought of opening them. Amaya put a hand on Magdalys's, steadying it. Together they opened the file.

GIVEN NAME: MAGDALYS ROCA (MARGARET ROCHEFORD)
BORN: JANUARY 4, 1851
PLACE OF ORIGIN: MATANZAS PROVINCE, CUBA
DELIVERED TO THE ASYLUM BY: HARRISON WEED, OF 893 MULBERRY STREET, MANHATTAN, NEW YORK
MOTHER: CARIDAD SAENZ LOPEZ SALAZAR
FATHER: SEÑOR PABLO GIBRALTAR MONSERRAT ROCA

And that was it. Neither alive nor dead, free nor enslaved. Just names on a piece of paper and some province of Cuba Magdalys had never heard of. And this strange man named Weed. His name showed up in the files of her sisters and brother (they all had the same father but four different mothers, Magdalys noticed), confirming what Magdalys had suspected: The mysterious tobacco-smelling, mustached man was Harrison Weed. And whoever he was, had not only stolen Magdalys's sisters away from her, but also dropped off Magdalys herself. He was the only link she had to her parents, then.

Mulberry Street.

Fine. Now she had one stop on her way out of New York.

She'd find out whatever she could from this Harrison Weed, and then she'd make her way down south to Montez. One way or another, she would do it. She just had to figure out how.

"The ferry!" Halsey Crunk yelled, startling everyone. "It's the ferry! Cymbie! Come quickly!"

Magdalys looked up from the files. Two dim lanterns danced across the water toward them like fiery ghosts. A long, curved sauropod neck cut a slender silhouette against the dark blue sky between them.

"Terribly sorry bout that," a voice called out in a thick Irish accent. "Got a bit held up dropping some cargo in Queens, you know, and then what with the riots and all we was a tad cautious on the return."

"It's alright!" Cymbeline called, running up to the shore. "We're just glad to see you. Come on, everyone, quickly now!"

The huge sauropod pulled up along the shore. A wooden platform had been constructed along its back, and the ferryman stood at the front of this holding a long rod that dipped into the river. "All aboard, then, laddies!"

Two Step and Sabeen boarded first. Mapper and Amaya went next, then Magdalys, and finally Halsey, Marietta, and Cymbeline. The planks were slippery, and it felt like at any moment the whole thing might just fall apart and leave them to sink beneath the surface. Or the sauropod might decide to dive beneath the surface, and well, that'd be that. Instead, the ferryman made some clucking noises and pushed them away from the shore with his rod. Magdalys thought of the other orphans, now refugees, and sent up a tiny prayer that they were safe somewhere. Then the ferry sauropod let out a gentle hoot and they were off, gliding smoothly across the black waters of the East River, the burning streets of Manhattan behind them and the darkness of Brooklyn ahead.

PART TWO

DACTYL HILL

CHAPTER TWELVE
MIDNIGHT AT THE BOCHINCHE

IT HAD PROBABLY just been a few hours, but by the time Cymbeline led them up to a rickety wooden door beneath a sign that said THE BOCHINCHE, Magdalys felt like they'd been walking the whole night.

Sleepy, darkened clusters of houses had given way to empty stretches of wilderness that had become winding streets, and then they were trudging up, up, up a long hill. Everyone stayed pretty quiet; the echoes of all that had just happened lingered like angry ghosts. As they approached the summit, dark shapes flitted across the sky above them, letting out occasional hoots and squawks in the night.

Dactyls, Magdalys realized. They didn't see many pteros except the little messenger ones in Manhattan — maybe because they were all over here. Seemed like the air was full of them. She could make out tiny little microdactyls, medium-sized minidactyls, and then the fully grown pterodactyls, all sailing back and forth, snapping at each other or whatever prey they could find, dancing across the darkness.

It was strangely comforting.

"Welcome to Dactyl Hill," Cymbeline had said, watching Magdalys's look of wonder at the soaring pteros.

A massive fortress-like building glared down at them from the top of the hill; torches lit either side of its huge front gate. "That's the Penitentiary," Cymbeline told them. "Keep your distance." And then she'd led them down a winding series of side streets and up to the Bochinche. She knocked once, paused, then twice more. The door swung open and a grinning face poked out. "Who — Cymbie? Oh my stars, girl! I was wondering where you've been! My goodness, girl, come in, come in!"

And in they went.

"That's not how it works, Louis!" a man in a top hat yelled as they shuffled in. He sounded like he was trying to act mean but couldn't help laughing instead.

Candles flickered on wooden tables in the dimly lit bar. A group of folks were gathered in the middle, playing cards and carrying on the way Magdalys and the kids at the orphanage did when none of the matrons were around.

"I didn't say it *works* like that," another man, Louis, said. He was short, a little older than the first man, and impeccably dressed. "I said that's how we gotta play it. Not the same."

Everyone laughed. Someone dropped another card and a collective groan went up.

A soft, tinkling melody rose from the far end of the room, where a figure in white clothes sat hunched over an old wooden piano. A few smudged windows let in the hazy glow of the gas lanterns out on the street. Magdalys noticed newspapers scattered around on the tabletops and a bookshelf along one wall, overflowing with hardcover novels.

"Come on, draw," someone said. "We don't have all night, D."

"Do I tell you how to play?" the man in the top hat retorted. "Clearly not, because then maybe you wouldn't be losing so bad."

Everyone shook their heads and rolled their eyes.

"Mr. Barrett," the woman who brought them in yelled. "Mr. Barrett! Go in the kitchen and fish up some milk, please. We have visitors and they're just babies, it seems."

Magdalys had to hold back from bristling. After all she'd been through in the past few hours, a baby was the last thing she felt like. But the smiles around her were friendly, and the place smelled like the living: a musty mix of sweat and smoke and whiskey — so much better than the grim, antiseptic emptiness of the orphanage.

Plus, she'd never seen so many people who looked like her

acting so fearless and free. Sure, black and brown folks gathered at the Zanzibar for shows and had a good ol' time at it too, but the shadow of what was outside always loomed. Even before it blew up into the nightmare tonight had become, Manhattan hadn't felt safe. Everywhere Magdalys turned, there was a reminder that she wasn't welcome, she was an outsider. But Manhattan was all she knew, so if she didn't belong there, where did she belong?

"Louis, if you don't stop dropping those aces, I swear, we fightin'."

"I wish you would come over here and make me stop."

"Boy . . ."

Maybe here, Magdalys thought, gazing at the laughing card players and the scattered smaller groups chatting at the bar behind them. *Maybe here in Dactyl Hill.*

"Hey!" the woman who brought them in yelled, even louder this time. "Did y'all hear me? I said we got babies in the house." Everyone got quiet and looked up. Magdalys felt the blood run to her ears. "So behave yourselves and pretend you're the good, proper citizens you masquerade as when you out and about on the boulevard, okay?"

"But, Bernice, we don't even —" the man in the top hat started, his face a mask of angelic innocence.

"Shut it, David."

The whole bar yelled, "Ohhh!"

Bernice led them through the crowd, which parted to either side of her like the Red Sea for Moses, and then she cleared some folks away from the bar so they could climb up on the stools. Glasses of warm milk awaited each of them, which Mr. Barrett had placed carefully down after making sure he had an accurate head count. Bernice nodded approvingly. "There you go, youngens, now drink up and rest yourselves while I have a chat with Ms. Crunk here."

They did as they were told, all a little too exhausted and in shock to do much else.

"And you!" Bernice hollered. "Halsey! What are you doing skulking in the corner? Who's that with you, Mr. Crunk? A white lady? Bring her over. Mr. Barrett will sort you out with some drinks. You look a mess, Halsey. You'll rest yourselves here or I'm not fit to run the Bochinche."

Halsey and Marietta waded through the crowd and found seats at the bar. Clearly, everybody's business was everybody's business at the Bochinche, Magdalys realized. The card game swung back into full-tilt rambunctiousness as Cymbeline and Bernice conferred in a corner by the piano.

"Of course," Bernice kept saying. "Think nothing of it . . ." and then, "As long as you like, Cymbie, you know that."

Magdalys couldn't make out what Cymbeline was saying, but it sounded like she felt bad about whatever she was asking and Bernice would have none of it.

"It's been empty for months," Bernice said. "Ever since, you know . . . Of course, Cymbie, of course. Oh, stop! And anyway . . ."

Then Cymbeline spent a few minutes explaining

something in a hushed voice — probably the events of the night. Partway through, Bernice cut her off and called for David and Louis to come listen. They crossed the room with long strides, both their faces creased with concern.

"Mr. Ballantine, Mr. Napoleon, this is Cymbeline Crunk, Shakespearean act —"

"Miss Crunk!" Louis bowed low before Bernice could finish talking. "It is an honor. Your performance of Lady Anne was breathtaking. The name's Louis Napoleon. No relation to the diminutive temperamental French emperor, I'm afraid."

Cymbeline stood there gaping for a few moments, then offered her hand for the short, dapper man to kiss.

"Mr. Ballantine and Mr. Napoleon are coordinators with the Vigilance Committee," Miss Bernice explained, "which helps fugitive slaves make it farther up north and works to stop the Kidnapping Club from sending our folks south to bondage."

"Of course." Cymbeline looked a little awestruck. "It's an honor to meet you both. I've been following all your work in the papers, and . . . Well, it's truly an honor."

The papers? Magdalys thought. *Whoa.*

"I'll have to catch a show one day," David said, kissing her hand when Louis was done.

"You'll have to wait till we rebuild our theater, I'm afraid. It burned down in the riots tonight."

"Riots?" David said, suddenly all business.

Louis looked stricken. "Tonight?"

Cymbeline nodded. "They torched the Colored Orphan Asylum as well. These kids are only here because they were at our show when it happened."

"My god!" Bernice gasped. The rest of the bar had gone quiet now; everyone stood and began gathering slowly around.

"And there's more. Riker is out on raptorback with the Kidnapping Club."

"Riker!" David snarled.

"They tried to snatch these guys from me, but we got away on a fire brigade brachy. I don't know what happened to the other orphans though."

David sprang into action. "Louis," he commanded. "The courthouse, quickly. The night court should still be open downtown, unless the riots shut it down." Louis was already pulling on his jacket. "Get a writ of habeas corpus for each orphan," David went on, more thinking out loud than instructing Louis, who clearly already knew exactly what to do. "That'll help us get legal custody to keep 'em safe. But we'll need the names of each of them . . . There must be at least a hundred?"

"One hundred and eighty-one," Marietta said, stepping out of the shadows. She looked even more bedraggled and busted up than Magdalys had realized, but her fists were clenched.

David looked up. "Oh? And who are you?"

"Marietta Gilbert Smack, sir. I am — was — a matron at

the orphanage. One hundred and eighty-six minus these five. And I know their names. At least, eighty-nine percent of them. I made myself commit them to memory, you see. During the overnight shift. But I wasn't quite finished memorizing when . . . tonight happened."

Everyone just stared at her for a moment.

"I'll go with you, Mr. Napoleon," Marietta said.

"Good," David said. "Louis, go on dactylback, it'll be faster."

Marietta's eyes went wide. "D-dactyl . . . back?"

Magdalys perked up. She had heard rumors about people riding pteros, but she didn't really believe them, and Dr. Sloan's Dinoguide definitely advised against it in bright red letters. She'd always wanted to try . . .

Louis looked amused. "That a problem, ma'am?"

Marietta firmed up her face and shook her head. "Not at all. I'm ready when you are."

Louis nodded once, then took off out the door. Marietta waved goodbye to the kids, thanked Cymbeline, and then followed him out.

Everyone looked back at David, who took off his top hat and round spectacles and shook his head. "Gonna be a long night," he said. "I can't believe we didn't hear until now."

Gonna be? Magdalys thought. She couldn't imagine how the night could possibly get any longer.

"I know, dear," Bernice said. "I know."

David stood. "Miss Bernice, send a dactyl if you hear anything else." He nodded at Magdalys, who realized she had been staring intently at him, then headed for the door. "The rest of y'all, arm up and meet me back here in twenty. If you have dinos, ride 'em. Let's move."

"Can I help?" Cymbeline asked.

David turned slowly, shook his head. "You've done enough tonight, my dear. You've done so much. Rest now. There'll be plenty more to do tomorrow, that I promise." And then he was gone.

Cymbeline looked somehow crestfallen and relieved at the same time.

Magdalys had no idea what they were up to, but even through her exhaustion, she desperately wanted to know. They were *doing* something. Probably were about to head right into the mess that she and the others had just escaped. Who were these strange, amazing people? Between them and Cymbeline, Magdalys felt like she'd discovered a whole new kind of saint over the course of the night, these brilliant, fearless heroes who looked like her and were ready to do anything to make the world what it should be instead of what it was.

Before she could ask about David and Louis, Bernice and Cymbeline picked up the beer bottles that Mr. Barrett had left on the bar for them and clinked them together. "It's settled then," Bernice said, a sad smile on her face.

Cymbeline was smiling too, though the wear and tear of the night could be seen all over her tired face. They took long swigs, and then Bernice turned to the bar. "Kids, let me show you to your rooms."

Two doors faced each other at the end of a dim hallway on the second floor of the Bochinche. The boys and Halsey filed into the one on the right; Bernice showed Magdalys, Amaya, Little Sabeen, and Cymbeline into the one on the left.

"It's a little cramped, I'm afraid," Bernice cooed. "But you know, we can spruce it up for you tomorrow and make it nice. Not to worry. For now, rest, little dearies. And you too, Cymbie. You've had a long night. Washroom's down the corridor to the right. Holler if you need anything. There's extra bedding in the dresser."

It was a little cramped, and none of them cared.

"We'll figure out your new lives in the morning," Bernice said, closing the door as she slipped out. "Not to worry."

New lives? Magdalys thought. She wasn't sure what it meant, but somehow she liked the sound of it.

For a moment, they all just stood there in the sudden silence. "You're not going home, Miss Cymbeline?" Sabeen asked.

Cymbeline shook her head. "My brother and I lived upstairs from the theater." Her voice cracked. She stared at the floor. "I have no home."

Sabeen wrapped her arms around her waist, and Cymbeline stroked the girl's hair idly.

"Thanks for saving us," Magdalys said.

Amaya nodded. "We would all be dead or kidnapped if it wasn't for you."

Cymbeline laughed but her eyes were watery. "You guys saved me as much as I saved you, trust. Anyway, it's been a long night." She placed her shotgun on the dresser with a loud clunk. "Enough cutesy stuff, let's go to bed."

Amaya blew out the lantern. Then, the three girls and Cymbeline stripped down to their underclothes and crawled into the single bed, each making room for the next as they huddled close.

Cozying up between Amaya and Cymbeline, Magdalys felt some of the heaviness that had been perched on her tired heart just drift away. Shelter. Somewhere to rest. Somewhere safe. She began fading to sleep with a slight smile on her face.

Then, one by one, the faces of the other kids from the Colored Orphan Asylum cycled by: Ray Sampson, who told Sabeen stories at bedtime; Bernadette and Syl, who everyone thought were sisters even though they hadn't even known each other before coming to the orphanage; Sweety Mae, who made fun of everyone else, in spite of her name.

Magdalys wasn't that close with most of them, but she'd come to rely on their faces, their smiles and pouts and quirks and annoyances, as part of her daily life.

And now she'd probably never see them again.

Worse than that, they might be on their way down south to some horrible fate. Why had Magdalys and the others been saved? Just because they'd been at a play that night? It seemed so random and unfair.

Then, from somewhere far away, she heard the gentle strains of an old voice humming, the swish of a broom, and the squeak of Mr. Calloway's well-shined boots echoing across the marble floor.

Magdalys felt her own tears land on the pillow as she drifted off to sleep.

CHAPTER THIRTEEN
A DAPPER MORNING

"WHOA," MAGDALYS SAID, looking up from the sweet oats and coffee that Mr. Barrett had put in front of her without a word when she'd come downstairs at daybreak.

The boys had transformed overnight. Two Step wore a dapper three-piece pinstripe suit, complete with shiny buttons and a bowler hat. He still had his orphanage shoes on, and it looked like the suit might be a couple sizes too small, but he looked terrific. Mapper stood beside him in the stairwell doorway, wiping his glasses on his sleeve and arching an eyebrow; he was decked out in loose overalls and a way-too-big white button shirt. A paperboy cap sat on his hair, which he'd gelled into a tall tower sticking straight up off his head. Someone had even shaved down the sides for him.

They stood perfectly still for a couple seconds, letting Magdalys stare in wonder, and then Mapper sauntered in one direction while Two Step, of course, broke into a sly two step, shimmying and shaking his way around the table.

"Uh . . ." Mr. Barrett said. "You boys want breakfast?"

"Quite quite, good sir," Two Step said, sashaying behind Magdalys while Mapper strutted around from the other direction.

"Indeed indeed," chortled Mapper.

"What on earth?" Magdalys demanded. They both slid into chairs on either side of her.

"Just getting spiffy for our morning constitutional, you know," Two Step said.

"Quite quite," Mapper added.

Mr. Barrett put two bowls of sweet oats on the table and walked off, shaking his head.

"Halsey found a trunk of cool clothes in our room," Two Step confided, finally back in his normal voice. "So he decked us out and did Mapper's hair."

"Wow," Magdalys said. "You guys had a real-deal slumber party."

"Don't be mad because we're more fashionable than you," Mapper chided around a mouthful of oats.

"Oh, I'm not," Magdalys. "Trust me."

"But how are you going to dactyljump from roof to roof sweeping chimneys if you're dressed like proper gentlemen?" Bernice said, walking in from the back room.

Mapper, Magdalys, and Two Step stood up at the same time. "We're doing what now?" Magdalys gaped.

"They're still clashing at Gettysburg," Mr. Barrett said, walking back in with a newspaper in hand. "Sounds bad." He passed it to Bernice, who squinted at the page and shook her head.

"What happened?" Two Step asked.

Magdalys was only half there, though. The other half was soaring through the Brooklyn skies on dactylback. *The pterodactyls,* Dr. Barlow Sloan's Dinoguide declared, *are a feisty and skittish bunch. They can be subdued and ridden, even in the wild, but it's usually helpful to startle them first. And they often swoop in unpredictable and startling directions, just to have a laugh at their rider's expense. And sometimes that expense winds up being a shattered skull.*

"Lee's army pressed further into Pennsylvania," Mr. Barrett said, pouring coffee into a ceramic mug and passing it to Bernice. "They figure if they can make it all the way to Washington, well, that'd be a wallop and a half for the morale of the Union."

"And they're right," Bernice added without looking up from the paper.

"Mhm," Mr. Barrett grunted. "At least General Grant has shown some grit down at Vicksburg."

General Grant. Magdalys snapped back to the world of walking on the earth. Montez's mounted trike battalion was assigned to Grant's army. What had happened? Immediately, her mind filled with images of Montez laid out on a cot somewhere, wasting away as gray-clad soldiers stormed over barricades.

"And if this new General Meade turns out to be anything like the last couple hickjops Lincoln's put in charge, well . . ." Mr. Barrett shook his head. "Even if he whups 'em at Gettysburg, he'll just sit on his hands twiddling about in the Pennsylvania rain until Lee regroups and has another go at it."

"And if he doesn't whup 'em?" Mapper asked.

Bernice and Mr. Barrett traded an uneasy glance.

"Things'll get very dire indeed, I'm afraid," Bernice said. "And they're already pretty bad, as you yourselves saw last night."

"How do we look?" Sabeen said, posing in the doorway with an elegant gown that was about four sizes too big. She even had lavish fake silk gloves and a humongous sun hat. Cymbeline appeared behind her, also fully decked out in evening wear.

Amaya came downstairs and ducked past them, still in her plain orphanage dress. "Utterly ridiculous," she muttered, shaking her head.

"Amazing!" Two Step and Magdalys said together, standing up and applauding.

"Completely unprepared for the day ahead," Bernice chided. "But also utterly adorable."

Sabeen and Cymbeline curtsied at the same time.

Bernice started scooping sweet oats out of a big iron pot into bowls. "Now everybody eat up and then go change into clothes you won't mind getting covered in soot and dactylpoop."

"Dactylpoop!" Mapper and Two Step exclaimed.

CHAPTER FOURTEEN
ROOFTOP DACTYLS

"AND GO!" LITTLE Sabeen yelled.

Magdalys, Two Step, and Mapper, now all in street clothes, charged across the rooftop, full speed. Up ahead, a squad of dactyls huddled at the edge of the building, sunning themselves and chattering in shrill squawks.

"This seems like the worst idea in the world," Two Step pointed out, already out of breath.

"Maybe it is," Magdalys said, but she couldn't keep the smile from breaking out across her face. "But it's the only way to get across."

"Maybe getting across is overrated," Mapper suggested from a little behind them.

Magdalys rolled her eyes. "We've already swept all the chimneys on this block."

"This is gonna sound ridiculous," Two Step said, "but we could always, you know, climb down the stairs like normal people and then walk across the street to the next block."

"And waste all that precious time?" Magdalys scoffed. "Please! Anyway, too late!"

They came up fast on the dactyl squad, just like Bernice had told them to do. "Dactyls are not the brightest pteros," she'd said while they finished the last of their sweet oats. "And some of those micro and mini ones are pretty weak, all told. But they're social. That means that to survive, they travel in a group. A group of dactyls is called a squad. That's why you see 'em all grouped up on those building tops like that. You just gotta find a squad, then pick one, get a good running start, surprise the pteropoop out of it . . ."

All five pairs of eyes went wide.

"Not literally, of course," Bernice added with a chuckle. "And then off you go!"

On either side of Magdalys, Mapper and Two Step were shaking their heads in horror.

"Just stay within the boundary lines of Dactyl Hill, please, and mind you don't go near that silo on the edge of town. Or the Penitentiary, for heaven's sake. And keep track of the chimneys you sweep so I can go charge them for it when you're done. Now finish your breakfast, kids. You have a long day ahead of you. And when the summer's over, we'll see about getting you enrolled in that African Free School they opened up over in Weeksville."

Now they were bearing down on the squad, and the dactyl Magdalys had picked was flapping its wings like it might be about to take off. Magdalys narrowed her eyes and ran harder, slamming into the dactyl's back and wrapping her arms around its neck like Bernice had said to do. An explosion of caws and shrieks erupted around her as two dozen wings started flapping at the same time. She felt herself plummeting and heard the dactyl screech. *Fly!* she thought, but even as she did, the buildings around them fell away and she and the dactyl soared toward the sky.

She glanced back, saw Two Step on top of another dactyl, screaming for dear life. Mapper stood on the roof, surrounded by flapping wings, shaking his head. Sabeen was a few feet behind him, watching in awe. The morning sun threw their shadows long across the rooftops.

And then all of Brooklyn stretched beneath Magdalys: the giant Penitentiary at the top of the hill, the neighborhoods rising and falling amidst the wilderness, the sun-soaked bay.

She released a yell of pure joy, felt the summer wind kiss her face and play with her hair.

And this dactyl — this strange and beautiful creature with its wrinkled, gray-brown hide, barrel chest, and slender neck — she wanted to hug it. Bernice had told them to use the crest extending from the back of the dactyls' heads to nudge them one direction or the other, but this one had already responded to her thoughts just like the brachy had, and Magdalys had no intention of yanking its head around if she didn't have to.

Up, she thought, and the reply in her mind sounded something like *fubba fubba fubba fubba*. It was real, this connection. She wasn't making it up. Maybe she'd always had it, but had never gotten a chance to let it manifest — it's not like she'd been able to spend much time with dinos up till now, and when she did, she certainly didn't try to communicate with them. Or maybe this was a new skill that had developed somehow. Either way, it was the greatest gift she could imagine. And she was absolutely sure no one would believe her if she tried to explain it. They'd probably lock her up in a whole other kind of asylum. No. The world wasn't ready for Magdalys's special abilities. It would be her secret with the dinos.

Fubba fubba fubba fubba, sang the dactyl.

They soared even higher and then careened in a wide circle toward the shipyards at Red Hook, filled with boats of all kinds and the long necks of sauropods off-loading crates, and then back around toward Dactyl Hill.

That tree-lined neighborhood at the top of the smaller slope must be the Crest, Magdalys thought, where all the affluent Brooklynites were said to live, promenading along the streets astride their graceful duckbills. An elegant dome punctuated the cluster of official-looking buildings in downtown Brooklyn, and there was the wide stretch of Flatbush Avenue that ran from the ferry terminal up to the top of Dactyl Hill.

Then, suddenly, they were sinking again, and the building tops rushed up toward Magdalys as the two plaits Sabeen had braided her hair into that morning flapped behind her in the rushing wind. *Fubba fubba fubba foooooooo!* came the strange muttering in her mind. The dactyl was diving.

"Don't stay on 'em long," Bernice had offered as a final warning. "Most of the untrained ones are not that strong and can't hold your weight for much time. Just get to the next rooftop and let 'em free. One thing there'll always be more of on Dactyl Hill is dactyls."

Right. In the wonder of seeing the whole world from above for the first time, Magdalys had forgotten that part. The rooftops got bigger and bigger and Magdalys was pretty sure she was about to get dashed across them and splattered to a million pieces when the dactyl swooped low over the chimneys at the last second and then came in for a bumpy landing, stopping right at the building edge. Magdalys hopped off and teetered back and forth for a few seconds, trying to remember what gravity felt like.

"Thank . . . you . . ." she stuttered. The dactyl squawked twice in what might've been a snicker, and took off to join its squad.

Magdalys scanned the rooftops for her own squad. She caught sight of Two Step still screaming his head off on dactylback not too far away. "Over here," Magdalys called, laughing. "Two Step!"

He stopped screaming long enough to see her, then veered his ptero toward the rooftop where she stood waving. They landed in a tangled crash and then Two Step popped up with a huge smile on his face. "That was *amazing*!"

"Didn't sound like you were having much fun," Magdalys pointed out.

"I mean, it was terrifying but whoa! Whoa."

Magdalys shook her head. "You're a mess, Two Step, you know that?"

He shrugged. "Where's Mapper?"

"Don't think he made it off the rooftop. He was watching from the edge when I looked back."

"I don't blame him," Two Step said. "That was the scariest thing I've done since . . . well, since last night, when I did about five hundred scary things I never thought I'd do."

"Good point," Magdalys said.

"What we do now?"

"Sweep the chimneys, I guess." She pulled the brush-extending pole out of her satchel. "Let's do it."

By the time the sun started setting over the Manhattan skyline in the distance, Magdalys and Two Step were covered in soot, but they'd gotten the whole process down to a smooth, step-by-step rhythm. Hop to a rooftop, spread out to opposite ends and sweep each chimney until they met up in the middle, jump a dactyl to the next block and start it all again. They even made a game out of it; whoever swept the most chimneys got first pick from the dactyl squad and could decide which way they headed next.

A few times during the afternoon, Magdalys caught sight of Mapper and Sabeen jetting from roof to roof a few blocks away. They'd wave and shout insults back and forth about each other's flying skills, then get back to work.

"Think that's the silo Miss Bernice mentioned?" Two Step asked, gazing off toward a spiraling cluster of dactyls in the darkening sky to the east.

Magdalys brushed some soot off her overalls as she walked up next to him. A little beyond where the houses ended on the far side of Dactyl Hill, a towering concrete building stood surrounded by barren fields. It was round with no windows at all; a metal roof covered most of the opening at the top, but a gap could be seen leading into the depths. Hundreds of dactyls swarmed around it, diving in and out and fussing with each other.

"No idea," Magdalys said, taking a few steps back and letting a smile break out on her face that would tell Two Step exactly what was about to happen. "Guess we better find out."

"Aw, man! Mag-D, wait up!"

CHAPTER FIFTEEN

THE SILO ON THE EDGE OF TOWN

THE ROOFTOPS OF Dactyl Hill passed beneath Magdalys like a slow-moving parade. It was near nightfall on a simmering July Saturday, and all the horrors of the night before seemed to be whisked away on the rushing wind. Folks were out and about on the streets below; they milled about like tiny, fancy ants. Even from way up in the air, Magdalys could tell they were dressed up nice, promenading along the avenues in clusters and pairs, probably heading to social clubs and balls.

Then, very suddenly, a gray shadow seemed to pass over the world. The dactyl had taken her directly over the Penitentiary. The castle-like fortress stretched three whole city blocks along the summit of Dactyl Hill. Towers rose up at its four corners, each with narrow windows along the sides and a howitzer cannon perched at the top. Guards with shotguns marched on knuckleskull dinos along the tops of the wide walls. In the middle, various stone buildings clustered around a central yard with a platform in the middle: the hanging gibbet. Magdalys shuddered. She'd heard plenty of stories about black and brown people getting tossed within those stone walls for no reason at all. Being restricted to an orphanage had been bad enough; she couldn't imagine being locked in a cage with who knew what kind of actual criminals.

Up ahead, the sun dipped behind a hazy cloud bank and the world really did darken a few shades. And then they passed the Penitentiary and were soaring over open fields — cow pastures, Magdalys now realized. A few of the lumbering mammals stood grazing in the enclosures. Beyond that, the strange building loomed beneath what looked like a living tornado of dactyls.

"What you think it is?" Two Step asked, pulling up alongside Magdalys.

"No idea. But we're gonna have to land on it. These dactyls won't hold out much longer, and I don't wanna end up in those pastures."

Two Step nodded and they surged toward the spiraling flock.

The stench hit them like a wall of foulness about thirty feet out.

"Gah!" Two Step yelled, covering his nose with one hand while keeping a tight grip on his dactyl with the other.

Magdalys scrunched up her face. It smelled like the dead mouse they'd found in the orphanage one night, but times ten thousand. "Whatever this place is, it's no wonder they keep it on the outskirts of town."

The closer they got, the worse the funk became, until Magdalys felt like she was going to retch. Their dactyls came in for a jolty landing on the rim of the huge silo. The squawking swirl of pteros around them eclipsed the whole sky.

"Careful," Two Step said as Magdalys stepped up to the inner edge of the building and peered in.

"Fancy you saying that," Magdalys chided, but then a terrible moan rolled through her so suddenly she almost toppled into the hole. "Ah!"

"What's wrong?" Two Step asked, dashing over to steady her.

She shook her head, eyes closed. "It's fine, just . . ."

Arrrrrrrrrrrrroooooooooooooooooooooooghhhhhhhhhhhhh!!! it came again.

Magdalys felt like her heart was being torn to pieces each time the moan sounded. Like a sorrow was being born in her chest that was bigger than she was.

"Mag-D," Two Step said, his fingers tightening on her wrist. "Let's get out of here."

"Wait," she whispered. "Something's . . ."

Beneath them, a gigantic chain clinked, its jangly report echoing from the darkness. All the dactyls around them hurled into the air for a few moments in alarm, then came clamoring back down. The chain was fastened to a rusty platform at the far end of the rooftop. It twitched and shuddered, and the connecting link didn't look like it was nearly strong enough to hold whatever was pulling it.

"There's something big down there," Magdalys said. "A dino."

Oooooooooooooorrrrrrrrrghhhhhhhhhhhhh!!!! came the moan, and this time it sounded like it was pleading with her, begging for . . . something. Magdalys squinted through the heaviness of that call, tried to decipher its meaning.

Eeeeyyyyyoorggggghh!!

All she could think of was Montez. Montez with his nose in a book, being annoyed with all her questions but answering them anyway. Montez keeping an eye on Sabeen and the other little ones. Montez teaching everyone how to read after lights out, coming up with clever ways to remember the more complicated stuff.

Montez in a blue army uniform, trudging along toward battle with an old rifled musket, shoulders slumped.

Montez in a hospital bed somewhere, wounded. Or worse . . .

Aaaaaarrrrroooooooooghhhhh!!

The moan snapped Magdalys back to the world around her, the now-dark sky, the swarming dactyls. Two Step.

"Magdalys," he said softly. "We gotta go."

Even not knowing any of what she'd been thinking, going through, somehow Two Step understood. He understood that he didn't understand, and that was the most important thing of all. He knew enough to be tender with her without knowing why. If he'd tried to be pushy right then, she felt like she might've shattered.

Whatever was down in that circular prison, there was nothing she could do for it right now. Not right now. But maybe . . . maybe if it was something big enough and fierce enough, maybe it could help her get where she needed to go. She cast an apologetic glance at the darkness beneath them, whispered, "I'm sorry, whatever you are, that I can't help you," and then turned around and followed Two Step to a nearby squad of dactyls.

CHAPTER SIXTEEN
UPDATES AND RUMBLINGS

"HOW'D IT GO today?" Magdalys asked, setting her bowl of stew down and sitting on the bench beside Amaya. Around them, the Bochinche swarmed with rumors, tall tales, and nightmares about the Manhattan riots. David and Louis were nowhere to be seen, and that left everyone else to take wild guesses at all they didn't know.

"I heard the Feds been pulled back from the front to come handle the rioters."

"Psshh! Come on now. You think they give a damn bout us?"

"Ain't just about us, Mo. If these clowns resist the draft, who gonna fight?"

"I'd fight!"

"Go 'head, then."

"You know the riots comin' here next, right?"

"They can try. We ready."

Across the table, Two Step and Mapper chatted excitedly about their day while Sabeen ate quietly, her eyes glued to a book.

Amaya waved a hand in front of Magdalys's face. "Hello? How you gonna ask a question and then space out entirely when I'm answering?"

Magdalys shook her head. "Sorry! There's so much happening. Got caught up overhearing."

"You mean eavesdropping," Amaya said, but she had a slight smile as she slurped her stew. "Anyway, it was alright. Just worked the counter most of the morning, learned how their whole cash system works and how to make about half of the drinks."

"Whoa! That's a lot."

Amaya shrugged. "It's kinda interesting, I guess. Beats running from rooftop to rooftop on stinky ol' dinos." She scrunched up her face.

"Dactyls are pteros, not dinos, but anyway I didn't know you hate dinos!" Magdalys said.

"Heh, not everyone's like you, Mags. Give me a good old reliable machine over a nasty flesh-and-blood poop factory any day."

"Poop factory!"

"They poop a *lot* and you know it."

Magdalys covered her eyes. "That's not all they do though! They're amazing! And, like, today . . . They fly! Amaya, we flew today. It was . . . I've never . . ."

"You can keep it," Amaya said. Then she softened. "But I'm happy you had a good time. I do kinda wish I knew how to work 'em the way you do. It'd probably come in handy . . ."

Magdalys didn't ask what it would come in handy for in Amaya's imagination, but she had a feeling it wasn't just getting from place to place. "I could teach you," she said. "I mean, I could *try*," she added with a wink.

"Ha . . . there's definitely no guarantee. But yeah, I'd like that. Maybe I could teach you something in return?"

In her head, Magdalys saw Amaya's expert hands sliding the powder into the barrel of that pistol as the brachy thundered along down Fifth Avenue. "I'm sure I'll think of something." She smiled as she went back to her stew.

"Listen up everyone!" a familiar voice called out just as the simmer of excitement in the Bochinche reached its boiling point. "We got a lot to talk about and not much time, as usual, so gather round and keep the heckling to a minimum." It was David Ballantine, looking exhausted and bedraggled but still somehow dapper.

"How we sposta have a meeting if we can't heckle?" someone yelled. Someone else bapped him upside the head and everyone chuckled, but Magdalys could hear the nervousness creeping around the edges of their laughter.

"Was a long night; been a long day," David said. "The rioters still have control of most of the city." A general murmur of disappointment and anger. "Feds sposta be sending reinforcements, but you know . . . well, you know."

"Told ya," someone said, but no one knew or cared what it was he'd told.

"Plus they kinda busy with the whole dealing with a violent secession thing. On the plus side, I'm told the siege of Vicksburg is finally over — General Grant's raptor riders took the city early this morning after —" A huge cheer went up. David smiled, waiting for it to finish. "After a forty-seven-day standoff. Also a Negro division of mounted trike commandos apparently repelled a Confederate attack at a supply station called Milliken's Bend."

That was the fight Montez had been wounded in. "Did . . ." Magdalys started once the cheering had died down, but she realized she had no idea what to ask. "Have you heard . . . anything about what happened to the casualties?" Of course he hadn't. The whole thing was a big impossible void. The need to simply run out of there and just head south, south, south rose up in a frantic pulse through her body.

David shook his head. "Sorry, Magdalys. That kind of intel hasn't reached us yet. But if we hear anything at all, I'll let you know."

Magdalys nodded, trying not to let the tears well up and spill out of her.

"The assault at Milliken's Bend was the Rebs' last hope to get reinforcements to Vicksburg," David said over the excited chatter filling the Bochinche. "And the city fell shortly after, which means our boys dealt a decisive blow, fellas." More cheering. "We lost a lot of folks though. Seems they executed a number of prisoners and sold the rest into slavery." Moans and angry shouts. David unfolded a scrap of paper from his pocket. "Secretary of War Stanton apparently feels that, and I quote: 'the slave has proved his manhood.'"

The room seemed to let out a collective sigh of exasperation.

"Manhood?" someone grumbled.

"They said that a month ago when our folks got massacred at Port Hudson," someone else pointed out.

"How many people gotta die to prove to these fools what the rest of us already know?"

"I know," David said, shaking his head. "I know. And I don't know the answer. I just know we gotta keep fighting, on all fronts. Meanwhile, closer to home, dozens of our people been killed in the riots, and that's only what we know so far."

A collection of moans and gasps rose up.

"Details are still sketchy: Two down at the docks. At least five in midtown. Three in the Claw."

The room got very quiet. Magdalys thought of the sorrow she felt for Mr. Calloway, who she didn't even know that well, and tried to multiply it times a hundred and then again by eight. A well of rage and fear opened up inside her, bigger than anything she could imagine or understand, bigger than that brachiosaurus that had helped them, bigger than the world. She closed her eyes, felt Amaya's hand on her back, put her head on the older girl's shoulder.

"Mr. Napoleon is still looking into the situation at the Colored Orphan Asylum," David said after a few moments of silence. "From what he could gather, most of the orphans got away before the fire started. Seems an older gentleman who cleaned there held off the mob so the kids could escape."

Magdalys didn't realize she was crying until Amaya squeezed her shoulder.

"He was killed by the rioters," David said. "To the young folks we got here who knew him, I'm so sorry. We're doing what we can to make sure he receives a proper burial."

"What happened to the others?" Two Step asked. "You said *most* got away."

David shook his head. "We don't know. Yet. We're working on it. Dr. McCune Smith and Frederick Douglass already housed the ones that did make it out. Anyway, Louis is on it, so wherever the rest of the kids are, we'll find 'em. And he got lil' what's-her-name helping him out."

"Marietta," Magdalys said.

"Right! Thanks! That's it for now, folks. If you want to help, talk to Bernice at the bar; she's coordinating stuff right now. Kids . . ." David scanned the room, made eye contact with each of them. "Meet me in the back room when you're done eating, if you don't mind."

Amaya and Magdalys exchanged a glance. What on earth could David Ballantine want to talk to them about? Amaya squeezed Magdalys one more time and then let her go.

At the far end of the table, Halsey Crunk burped loudly. "Woe, destruction, ruin, and decay," he mumbled, nursing a beer. "The worst is death, and death will have his day."

CHAPTER SEVENTEEN
A SQUAD IS BORN

"LOOK," DAVID SAID, once Magdalys, Amaya, Sabeen, Mapper, and Two Step had all filed into the dim room across from the kitchen. The muted laughter and piano playing from the bar could still be heard through the wood-paneled walls.

"What's wrong?" Mapper asked.

Instead of finishing his sentence, David just sighed and shook his head as five pairs of eyes stared at him. "I just . . . I didn't want it to come to this."

"What can we do to help?" Magdalys said. "That's why we're here, isn't it?"

David nodded. "Of course it is. Because this ridiculous world has made soldiers of even our babies."

"We're not babies," Two Step said.

David smiled, sadly at first, then wider. "I know, it's an expression. One I just made up. And babies sounds better, right?"

"Sabeen's basically still a baby," Mapper said.

"Nuh-uh — I'm almost eleven!" Sabeen pouted. "I'm just small."

"Look," David cut in before anybody got rowdy, "we need your help. I hate asking you, because you should be playing with sticks and balls or whatever it is you young folks do for fun nowadays. But this is the world we live in, and with the riots, well . . . everything got a lot more dangerous and our resources are stretched way thinner. Every black New Yorker is in danger right now, and we need as many eyes on the street as we can get. You've all been given jobs, and yes, those are to earn your keep here at the Bochinche, but they're also important, um, strategically speaking."

"You want us to keep an eye out," Amaya said.

David looked relieved. "Exactly!"

"Holy crow!" Mapper yelled. "You want us to be spies!"

David, Magdalys, and Amaya all rubbed their eyes and groaned at the same time. "I mean . . ." David said. He adjusted his top hat and looked out the window; his hands moved in circles to explain better, but no words came out.

"Yes," Amaya finally said. "But if you *yell* that you're a spy, that means you don't get to be a spy anymore, because you've automatically failed the first test of being a spy."

"Aw, man!" Mapper said.

"This is the thing," David said, "here are all the people in this world you can trust." He held up both hands, palms out.

"Ten?" Two Step said. "Only ten people? Who?"

David shook his head. "That was meant to show that my hands are empty, Two Step. No people. You can trust no people in this world. That's how you have to act if you're going to be working for us. Understand?"

"We gotta trust you though, right?" Sabeen said. "Otherwise, what's the point? And who will we tell our information to once we collect it?"

"Okay, yeah, you got to trust me."

"Nice one," Mapper said, high-fiving Sabeen. "For a baby." Sabeen punched him in the shoulder and he snickered.

"We trust Cymbeline," Magdalys said. "She saved our lives."

"Well, yeah, I think Cymbeline's pretty trustworthy," David admitted. "And Louis and Bernice are definitely okay. But no one else! I mean it!"

They all stared at him.

"Except," he allowed after a moment, "and this is important: You have to trust each other. If you trust each other, it means you also have to be trustworthy to each other. You can't keep things from each other, not important things, not things about the work we're all doing. You can't be sneaking off, can't be lying. Not to each other. You are now the most important person in the world to four other people. That's all that matters. That's the only way this is going to work. You're a team."

Mapper perked up. "We're a team, you guys! I've always wanted to be on a team!"

"We need a name," Two Step said. "Teams have names."

David chuckled. "And that is my cue to exit! I'll leave you to it." He shuffled out of the room shaking his head.

"Dactyl Hill is where we're based out of," Magdalys said. "So we should be the Dactyl Hill something."

Mapper jumped to his feet. "The Dactyl Hill Dactyls!"

Everyone shook their heads.

"We're a squad," Two Step said slowly. "Remember what Miss Bernice said about dactyls?"

"That they're not very smart and can't carry you very far?" Mapper suggested doubtfully.

"That their poop takes forever to wash out of your clothes?" Sabeen tried.

"That to survive," Magdalys said, "they travel in a group." It was kinda corny, but Two Step had a point.

He looked at her with the biggest smile she'd seen on him since he found out about his parents. "Right! That there's big dactyls and minidacts and the tiny micro ones —"

"Like Sabeen," Mapper added. She shoulder-punched him again, this time hard enough to make him yelp.

"But the way they make it through the world is by sticking

together. That's why they stay flocking on the building edges in those big clusters."

Mapper, still standing, held his hands out to either side, smile ecstatic. "So we're the . . ."

"Dactyl Hill Squad!" everyone yelled at the same time. Even Amaya.

CHAPTER EIGHTEEN
ASSIGNMENTS, WARNINGS, AND A CODE

"WOW, WHAT'D I miss?" Cymbeline Crunk said, walking in with her eyebrows raised.

David came back in a few moments later, still shaking his head. "What indeed."

Cymbeline handed him a beer and propped herself against the table next to where he stood. Magdalys forced a smile. She had let herself get swept up in all the excitement, but not too much. She couldn't get attached. At least it wouldn't be them leaving this time, it would be her. Still, she could try to have fun in whatever little time she'd be around for.

"We a squad, Ms. Crunk!" Two Step yelled.

"The Dactyl Hill Squad," Magdalys added.

"And," Mapper said, "Mr. Ballantine asked us to —"

"Kyle Tannery!" Amaya snapped. "How are you so smart in almost every possible way except this most basic of things?"

Mapper's mouth dropped open. "You think I'm smart?"

"Anyway," David said with a chuckle, "Cymbeline already knows. I had to ask her permission before I spoke to you guys about it."

"Darn right," Cymbeline said, clinking her own bottle against David's. "I'm responsible for you guys now, I figure." Cymbeline was taking responsibility for them? That was pretty much the best thing Magdalys could imagine happening. "So anyone who wants to reach you has to get through me and my shotty first."

Everyone cheered.

"Alright, alright, guys," David said. "Let's get down to business for a sec, then you can go back to your squad party."

Folks got quiet in a hurry; being a squad, with a name and everything, had changed the game. They weren't just abandoned orphans anymore — they were part of something. They all felt it; Magdalys could tell from the focused hush that fell instantly over the room.

"The basic idea is, you each have your jobs — Magdalys, Mapper, Sabeen, and Two Step are on chimney sweep duty; Amaya is working the Bochinche. So that makes you the eyes and ears of the Vigilance Committee. If you see anything out of the ordinary or hear anything, you send word to Bernice via minidact. If you come across someone who looks like they are on the run, you let us know. If you see some unusual gatherings of folks, you let us know. I want complete coverage. A triceratops shouldn't be able to fart sideways without a message about it flapping its way back to the Bochinche. Clear?"

Amidst stifled laughs, the Dactyl Hill Squad nodded in unison.

"Now, thing number two is this: A lot of the Kidnapping Club's shenanigans go down in Manhattan, particularly by the docks. And by shenanigans, just to be perfectly clear, I mean they snatch African New Yorkers off the streets and send them down south to slavery. I know you've already had a run-in with the Club's boss, Magistrate Riker, so you know, as does Cymbeline, just how dangerous a group we're dealing with. This is not a game; it's not a joke. Lives are on the line, including every single one of yours. Is that clear?"

"Sir, yes sir!" the Dactyl Hill Squad responded as one.

The other orphans, Magdalys thought — they were out there in that cruel city somewhere while these monsters stalked the streets, waiting to snatch up anyone they could.

"So, we'll be taking shifts doing work in Manhattan; it's important right now because any kidnapped victims will probably be transported out through the docks. That's extra dangerous work, for obvious reasons. Unfriendly territory, and especially after the riots, we have fewer contacts there to get you out of a jam."

893 Mulberry Street, Magdalys's file had said. *Manhattan.*

That's where Harrison Weed lived, the man who had dropped her off at the Colored Orphan Asylum and stolen away her sisters. Her only hope of finding out more about her family.

"So," David said, "who wants to volunteer for the fir —"

Magdalys's hand shot up. "I do."

Everyone turned to stare at her.

"Well, alright," David said. "Good. We have contacts in a building down on Lispenard that can set you up to sweep some chimneys tomorrow morning. Who will join her?"

Magdalys elbowed Mapper. "Ow!" he snarled.

Sabeen raised her hand. Magdalys loved Sabeen, but she wouldn't be much help with what would have to be done.

She elbowed Mapper again. "What the heck?" he whispered, and then it dawned on him. "Oh! Uh, I'll go!"

"Alright," David said. "Magdalys and Mapper, then. Sabeen, you can go on the next run."

"Yes!" Magdalys said, trying to contain her excitement. She'd go to Manhattan, find Harrison Weed, and somehow get what she needed to know about her family from him. She'd have to figure out the how when she got there.

"But listen," David said, his voice turning stern again. "It's bad enough that we need to put you kids in the middle of this mess. So: You stay by the docks. You keep your eyes peeled for danger. Any trouble or if you get separated, you send word via microdact immediately. Clear?"

Magdalys and Mapper nodded.

"We have a few other agents embedded down there, including Napoleon. If they hear you're in trouble, they'll get to you. The hand sign is this . . ."

"Secret code hand signs?" Mapper squealed. Sabeen shook her head. "Could this possibly get any cooler?"

David rolled his eyes, then brought his left hand close to his chest and made a *V*, then a *C* with his fingers. "Got it? For Vigilance Committee." Everyone tried it. "Good. Look for it. Now Magdalys, Mapper, you head out in the morning after breakfast. Be extra careful and *no* unnecessary risks. Understood?"

"Completely," Magdalys said, gritting her teeth behind pursed lips.

That night, Magdalys lay in bed staring at the dark ceiling, her fingers laced behind the silky headscarf Miss Bernice had lent her. The caws of dactyls flying overhead mixed with Cymbeline and Sabeen's snores. Tomorrow she would have answers. They would be incomplete, surely, but they would be more than nothing, and nothing was basically what she had now, all she'd ever had.

She would find out *something*, and then, armed with that, she'd somehow get herself south, to New Orleans. She'd find Montez. She'd make sure he was alright, stay with him until he healed, and then together they'd go to Cuba and find their parents and sisters. They'd find them. The world might be broken, like David said, but maybe they could create their own sense of wholeness if they could pull their shattered family together again.

"You neither?" Amaya said, rolling over and lying on her back beside Magdalys.

Magdalys shook her head. "Too many thoughts."

"Same," Amaya said. "Everything got so real so suddenly in the past two days."

It wasn't like Amaya to admit that anything overwhelmed her, Magdalys realized. She almost never let her vulnerability show. "I feel like we've seen the best and the worst of this world in a very tiny amount of time."

They let the words sit in the dark air between them for a few moments, then Amaya said, "My father is a general."

Magdalys stayed quiet. If she prodded or acted too interested or fake in any way at all, Amaya would slip back into her shell like those little hermit crabs she'd read about and probably never come back out.

"He worked at a military school called the Citadel ever since I was little. And, of course, they didn't let me train. Everyone thought I was just cute. A little girl, and half Apache to boot, though they didn't really know what that meant. To them I was just a savage. But I was also the daughter of the great General Cuthbert Trent, and besides being a hero of the Mexican War, he was a head instructor there, so they couldn't mess with me too much. And my father trained me in secret, raised me a soldier, kept me on a strict military regimen, even taught me tactics and strategy, weapons . . . everything. And I knew, because I was who I was and because I was his daughter, I had to be good, so I wasn't just good; I was the best. Better than the best. And they had no idea . . ."

Magdalys nodded. She'd seen exactly how good Amaya was. It wasn't just that she knew how to shoot — strategy and battle came naturally to her; it was obvious.

"And I hated them all, but I loved the training. It was like finally getting to be what I was meant to be, somehow. Even though I was young and had no idea about the world. I just learned everything I could, all in secret. Then Lincoln got elected and there we were in South Carolina, a state in the middle of secession. Then the war broke out and we fled north so he could take command of a Union regiment and head right back down south to fight the very people he'd been training. He stuck me in the Colored Orphan Asylum. I guess he thought I'd be safe there. I don't know. But I hadn't heard from him since, and I . . . I didn't know how I felt about it. Still don't. But then Von Marsh said I had a letter from him yesterday and I . . . I just froze." She sniffled, didn't cry. "And now it's gone. I'll never get it back. And part of me doesn't even care; the other part, it's all the other part cares about. I don't know if I love him or hate him, or if I want him to come back for me. I'm just . . . here. I don't know what I want."

"What about your mom?" Magdalys asked.

Amaya just shook her head. The silence grew long.

"I got a letter from the front lines," Magdalys said, when she was sure there was no more coming. "About Montez. He got hurt in battle. He's . . . he's unconscious."

She felt Amaya's warm hand wrap around hers. "What are you going to do?" Amaya said eventually.

Magdalys shook her head. "I'm gonna go to him." She paused. "Somehow." It didn't seem like enough. "Soon," she added, wondering if Amaya understood. *Now,* her heart screamed. *Now!*

Just before Magdalys fell asleep, she heard Amaya turn over again.

"Do you think they're okay?" Magdalys asked. "The other kids from the Asylum."

Amaya sighed. "No."

CHAPTER NINETEEN
MISSION TO MANHATTAN

MAGDALYS AND MAPPER rose before dawn with the rest of the newly named Dactyl Hill Squad. After fried eggs and coffee, they said their goodbyes to the others and headed off through the still-dark streets of Brooklyn. They caught a transit brachy down Flatbush Avenue toward the river, clinging to the side stirrups amidst grumbling morning commuters of all colors and classes. Around them, the city seemed to yawn and stretch, waking gradually as the sun rose over sauropods and swooping dacytls, brownstones and church steeples and municipal domes. Vendors set up their shops, hocking everything from oven parts to bicycles to dinofeed and saddles. The smell of freshly baked bread filled the air as they passed Atlantic Avenue, but it was soon replaced by the sharp tang of the giant brachy turds that hadn't yet been swept away from the night before.

At the crossing station, they waited in line, paid their fare from the pocket change Bernice had handed them, and watched as two lanterns emerged from the gray mist over the water, then the long neck of the sauropod between them, followed by its barge-covered rump.

"All aboard for Manhattan docks!" a voice called out. Mapper's hand wrapped around Magdalys's as they shuffled up the gangplank with everyone else and stepped over the dark waters onto the ferry.

"You alright?" she whispered.

Mapper nodded. "It's just . . ."

He didn't finish, but Magdalys knew. She felt it too: Manhattan.

Even before the riots, the city felt like a cruel, unwelcoming place to be. Tragedy seemed to lurk around every corner, casting its shadow over any wrong turn or chance encounter. The buildings, gaudy superstructures and run-down tenements alike, all frowned out from their foundations; each presided over its lot of land like the old angry white man Magdalys had seen once, brandishing a shotgun in front of his little shack in the Claw to make sure no one stole the withered apples off a sad little tree in his front yard.

The ferry sauropod let out a low, bone-chilling moan into the misty morning sky and then set off across the river.

Mapper squeezed Magdalys's hand.

And now, the riots had given teeth to all those prickly feelings of discomfort. Thoughts of Manhattan now would always be a thin varnish on top of the image of Mr. Calloway's boots dangling in the firelit night.

They'd barely made it out alive, and already they were headed right back into the thick of it all: the docks.

"What if they try to snatch us?" Mapper asked, not even bothering to hide the shiver in his voice.

Magdalys shook her head. "We'll jack 'em up, just like Miss Cymbeline would do if they tried to snatch her."

That gave Mapper a slight smile, but then he frowned again. "But we don't have a shotty like Miss Cymbeline."

Magdalys made a throwaway sign with her hands. "Who needs a shotty when you got dinos? You know they pay special attention to me."

Mapper nodded.

"I'll sic a few raptors on anyone trying to snatch us and that'll be that. And anyway, don't forget we part of a crew now. And not just the Dactyl Hill Squad . . ." She turned in toward Mapper and made the *V* and *C* sign against her chest. "Remember?"

Mapper smiled widely now, made the sign back.

"You really think those cats would let us get shipped off down south?"

"Uh-uh. They got a whole organization in place to make sure that's not what happens."

"Exactly," Magdalys said. Case closed. *Still,* she thought as the shadowy Manhattan docks emerged from the mist. *Still* . . .

The ferry sauropod navigated between huge armored warships and around a steamboat before docking alongside an ancient wooden frigate with cannons poking out of either side.

"Think that's a pirate ship?" Mapper asked.

Magdalys shook her head. "If they are, they got a lot of nerve docking in New York Harbor looking all pirate-shippy like that."

They followed the crowd down the gangplank and onto the pier. Hundreds of people swarmed the docks, even at this early hour. A fish market was coming to life along the avenue, and the shouts of merchants mixed with the caws of seagulls and rumble of steamboats coming in to port.

"Lispenard Street," Mapper said, squinting at the wild, ever-changing atlas of New York City he had stored inside his brain. "Lispenard Street."

Magdalys could tell that just having a task to do made all his earlier worries seem to fade away. She concentrated on keeping an eye out for any of Riker's Kidnapping Club goons and followed along as he guided them away from the docks and into the hustle and bustle of downtown Manhattan.

They headed up Church Street, a wide avenue crowded with businessmen in top hats and beggars and fancy ladies in wide skirts. "Victory at Gettysburg!" a newspaper seller yelled. "The Rebs routed all across the south as Vicksburg falls to Grant!" (*Was Montez there somewhere . . . somewhere . . .*) "Lincoln declares that the father of waters again goes unvexed to the sea! The Mississippi is in Union control! The Confederacy is cut in half and the New York rioters were routed overnight by federal troops!"

Magdalys wasn't sure if she believed him entirely — the man sounded like he was trying to sell her an aging dino as if it were a newborn — but the streets bore no sign of the rioting aside from a few covered-up windows that had been smashed and one burnt-out pharmacy. Other than that, everyone was milling about like it was just another day downtown.

Which, Magdalys figured, it pretty much was if you hadn't watched your only home become a charred wreckage and seen someone you cared about swinging from a noose just a day and a half ago.

They passed the Municipal Trade Bank, a huge, elegant fortress with marble pillars and an iguanodon-mounted guard on either side of the mighty doorway. A beggar shuffled in front of it, then dove out of the way as a dark purple stegosaurus trundled by, nearly trampling him, bags of mail and packages flapping at its flanks. A flock of microraptors chased a rat across the street, which was then scooped up by a policeman's knuckleskull and gobbled.

"Should be . . . here!" Mapper said triumphantly. They'd

turned onto a smaller side street and now stood in front of a large wooden door.

"Nice work, man!" Magdalys said. She'd been lost in thought again, hadn't even been scanning their surroundings like she should've been. She glanced around, saw no sign of any lurkers, and then stepped up and knocked twice with the big brass ring.

A few moments later, the door creaked open and Louis Napoleon peeked out and looked around. He squinted at Mapper for a few seconds, then broke into a huge grin. Magdalys glanced over; Mapper was making the *V* and *C* signs over and over on his chest, mouthing out the letters, and wiggling his eyebrows like a fool.

"Kids!" Louis said in a raspy, laughter-tinged voice. "Come on in!"

CHAPTER TWENTY
MANHATTAN SKYLINE

ALL AROUND THEM, Manhattan stretched out in rowhouses, great majestic cupolas, church steeples, and glowering government domes. The fierce July sunlight streamed in over a gray cloud bank and lit up the New York Harbor like a fire was rising from its depths. Magdalys took it all in with a sigh. It was beautiful, this city, but the weight of all she was about to do heavied up her thoughts and sent her heart racing.

Louis Napoleon had led them up a flight of stairs, down a corridor past a room alive with the thunk, hum, and tremble of a printing press, then up another flight and then another.

"There'll be a few dactyls up there," he'd said, opening a door to the bright rooftop. "We made sure of it. Aren't many of the bigger ones on this side of the river, but they're around here and there. You shouldn't have a problem getting from building to building."

Magdalys and Mapper thanked him and headed out into the sunlight.

"And remember, eyes open," Louis called before closing the door.

"Shall we start?" Mapper asked, walking up beside Magdalys and taking in the rolling rooftops around them.

"Which way is Mulberry?" Magdalys asked.

"Huh?"

"893 Mulberry, Mapper. That's where we're going."

"I thought —"

Magdalys hit him with her this-is-not-a-joke glare.

"You didn't just insist on me coming with you because we're friends, did you, Mag-D?"

"I mean, that was definitely *part* of it!"

Mapper shook his head. "David said no messing around! No unnecessary risks!"

"Mapper, look —"

"We sposta watch the docks. That's it. Sweep the chimneys and watch the docks. How you gonna have a whole address you planning to go to and you didn't even tell no one?"

"Mapper."

"Don't *Mapper* me, Magdalys. The *whole* thing is we supposed to trust each other. We a squad. You think that was a joke?"

"No, I —"

"How I'm supposed to trust you when you can't even tell me what the super secret side mission we on is about?"

Magdalys blinked. Mapper didn't want to disrupt the scheme, he just wanted to be in on the scheme. And anyway, he was right: They were a squad now, and she was going to have to start taking that seriously. Super secret side mission or not, it wasn't fair to make people come along on some shenanigans they didn't even know they were signing up for. She nodded, making a face. "You right, Mapper. I'm . . . I'm sorry."

Mapper stared. "And?"

"And I'm trying to bust into the house of a man named Harrison Weed who brought me to the orphanage and took my sisters back to Cuba so I can find out more about my family."

Mapper pumped his fist in the air. "*That's* what I'm talking about!"

"Whoa. I wasn't expecting that response."

Mapper was already heading for the nearest dactyl. "What are you waiting for? The 800 block of Mulberry Street is this way!"

"Whewee!" Mapper yelled as they landed their dactyls on a tar rooftop a few blocks away. "These Manhattan dactyls don't mess around."

"You really think that was any different than the Brooklyn

ones?" Magdalys asked, cracking her neck and stretching her arms out.

"Maybe it's just a different feel because the city's so much denser and doesn't have all that open space like in Brooklyn. I dunno. Anyway, should be" — he closed his eyes, took a few steps in one direction, stopped, walked over and then forward a few more steps — "right about . . . here!"

"So, that chimney?" Magdalys asked, her heart rate kicking up again.

"I think so . . . Yeah. Definitely. I'm sure of it."

"Okay, I'm going in."

Mapper held up both hands. "Hold up, sis. We need, like, a . . . a plan or something, right? I mean, we're not only breaking and entering into some random rich guy's fancy Manhattan apartment, we're doing it against the direct orders of the awesome club of awesome folks that we just joined. So, like, let's not mess this up?"

"Right," Magdalys conceded. There she went again already, not thinking like a team player. She would have to do better. "Okay. I go in, snoop around, find what I need, and if I'm not back out in, let's say, twenty minutes, you come in too. Yeah?"

"No offense, but that's a really basic plan, Mag-D. I mean, do you know what you're looking for?"

"Info . . . about . . . my family?"

"Right, but like, a file? A map? A guy who you're going to hang out the window till he tells you what you wanna know?"

"I mean, all of the above?"

"And secondly, what if you go down there and someone shoots you, and then what? I go down and get shot too? Bad plan."

"You got a better one?"

It was Mapper's turn to concede the point, but he did so as if he'd somehow won the whole argument. "Nope! But I'll figure one out while you're down there, I promise!" He flashed a winning grin.

Magdalys just shook her head as she climbed into the chimney. "I just hope you don't actually think you make any sense, Mapper. That's all."

"Good luck!" Mapper called as she lowered herself into the darkness.

CHAPTER TWENTY-ONE

THE NOT-SO-HUMBLE ABODE OF MR. HARRISON WEED

NO ONE HAD cleaned this chimney in a long time, Magdalys decided. She felt the thick layers of ash coating her hands and knees as she worked her way along down the narrow chute. As usual, the whole world became an eternal darkness soon after she got on her way. There was always a terrifying moment of emptiness when that happened: What if she got trapped in there and no one came to get her? What if some fool decided to start a fire and she got smoked out or burnt to a crisp? Then she'd take a breath — not too deep or she'd end up coughing till she heaved — and remind herself that every chimney let out into a fireplace and if she had to she could haul butt back up double time and be out of there.

This particular one did seem extra long, though. She tried not to think too much about it, just kept climbing down and down and down until finally a shard of light appeared beneath her.

She allowed herself a long exhale and then scaled the rest of the way down, landing with a muffled thud in the fireplace.

The dining room she stared out into was one of the most elegant places she'd ever seen. Fine linen cloth covered the table, which displayed eight porcelain dishes with perfectly placed silverware and folded napkins on either side. Even the curtains were magnificent! They were great, shiny, royal-looking ones with golden trim and tassels.

Magdalys stifled a gasp. Who was this Harrison Weed, with his fancy Manhattan apartment and strange dealings with Cuban orphans?

Whoever he was, he almost certainly had an office somewhere in here, and in that office would be his personal papers. And there, hopefully, Magdalys would get some answers.

She brushed as much soot off herself into the hearth as she could and then crept out of the fireplace, through the dining room — careful not to touch *anything* — and out into the carpeted hallway. Paintings of old white men adorned the walls, and here and there an ancient-looking bust of someone with a beard stared emptily from an inlet. The next room was a bedroom; beyond that was a washroom and a sitting area of some kind. At the far end of the corridor was a closed door. There was no way to open it without getting the shiny golden doorknob covered in black soot, but Magdalys hadn't come all this way just to give up because she was going to dirty up a rich man's apartment. She wiped her hand a few times, then turned the knob and walked in.

Bingo.

Thick books lined all the walls and cluttered a mantelpiece overhanging another fireplace. An elaborate wooden desk took up almost half the room, papers covering it like autumn leaves. She crossed the length of the room at a run and, not even bothering to try and keep them clean, started rifling through the stacks and stacks of documents.

Within just a few minutes, Magdalys had gone from irritated to disappointed to bored to furious, and now she was sliding quickly toward despair. The man had so many papers and none of them made much of any sense at all! There were records and info sheets full of scratched-out numbers and random words that didn't seem to have any rhyme or reason. It could be a code, Magdalys figured, but it wasn't one she'd be able to figure out any time soon, if at all.

She kept digging, frustration gnawing away inside her, until a single word on a folded-up parchment caught her eye.

It had clearly been delivered by microdact; those telltale claw imprints gave that away. And someone had written it hastily, that was for sure. Ink splotches speckled the edges of the paper, and the handwriting looked like it had been scribbled on dinoback.

Orphans was the word that brought Magdalys's frantic paper shuffle to a sudden halt. At the top, an elaborate circular seal glistened off the page. It had what looked like rays of light bursting out of a roaring tyrannosaurus in the center, and the words "K of the G C" were scrawled around the circumference. It was the same insignia that Riker had on the medallion he wore! And it glared off the tops of a bunch more of Weed's papers too. But what was the K of the G C?" Magdalys read:

> MY BROTHER KNIGHT — I TRUST ALL IS WELL WITH YOUR ENDEAVORS AND I WRITE YOU WITH THE UTMOST URGENCY.
>
> SHIPMENT OF 40 ORPHANS FROM THE COA FOR TRANSPORT SOUTH.
>
> WILL DELIVER AT 11 TONIGHT FOR IMMEDIATE REMOVAL FROM CITY LIMITS.

Magdalys gasped. The paper had today's date on it. In a little over twelve hours, they were sneaking the orphans out of the city.

> HAVE EVERYTHING READY ON THE DCARRION.
>
> IF THE CAPTAIN GETS ANTSY AGAIN, HANDLE HIM.
>
> WITH GREAT HASTE,
>
> R

Magdalys's eyes went wide. "Riker!" she said out loud.

Then the door opened and the tallest woman Magdalys had ever seen walked in and screamed.

CHAPTER TWENTY-TWO
CAUGHT!

"**WHAT ON EARTH** are you doing here, you filthy child?" The woman was dressed in a servant uniform and had tightly clenched fists, mahogany skin, and a French accent.

Magdalys tried to do the innocent-child face that Sabeen had perfected, but she was pretty sure it wasn't working. "I — I'm sorry, ma'am. I was starving and have nothing to eat, so I snuck in here thinking maybe —"

"Enough!" the woman screeched. "Look at this filth!" She swung her arm toward the open door, through which Magdalys could see the trail of soot and coal she'd left like bread crumbs. She'd tried to be so careful!

"I'm so sorry, ma'am! I can —"

"You can do nothing! How am I supposed to clean this up

before Mr. Weed gets back, hm? How? And look!" She stormed across the room so fast Magdalys had to dive out of her way before she trampled right over her. "The papers! Mon dieu!"

"I didn't mean to —"

The woman whirled around. "Did not *mean* to? You are covered in soot! You have come down the chimney! And now you are looking through Mr. Weed's papers? This is not a pantry. You are not stupid, child." Her eyes narrowed. "What are you up to?"

Magdaly's mind went irretrievably blank. "I just . . . I'm just . . ."

The woman seemed to make a split decision and whirled back to the blackened papers. "No matter! What matters is this filth that I 'ave to clean up! How to explain this to Mr. Weed, eh?" She gathered up the soot-covered papers, black clouds poofing into the still office air, and headed for the fireplace.

"Wait!" Magdalys called. "What are you doing?"

"Oh, child, there is no way I will be able to clean these, so I must burn them. Better that they don't exist at all than for Mr. Weed to think I was going through his things." She dumped them in the hearth and grabbed a book of matches from the mantelpiece.

"No!" Magdalys yelled, crossing the room at a run. She dove into the hearth, snatching up all the papers in her arms. If she had to, she'd scale the chimney, but it wouldn't be easy with her arms full. She started shoving them into her satchel.

"Mon cherie, you are going to 'ave to do better than that if you are a spy, I am afraid. Now come, get out of there and give!" — she yanked on Magdalys's satchel — "Me!" Another yank. Magdalys held on tight. "Ze! Papers!"

From somewhere far away, Magdalys heard a yell. It sounded like a boy. In fact, she realized as it got louder, it sounded like Mapper. The woman turned and yelled, "Mon dieu!" Then a terrific shattering sounded from the far wall and a huge dactyl burst through the window and landed on the desk, Mapper grinning triumphantly on its back.

"Filthy dino!" the woman yelled. "'Ow am I going to — !?" She backed up against the far wall and threw her arms up in disgust.

"Mapper!" Magdalys yelled, half laughing, half about to cry. "How — what . . . even?"

Mapper shrugged. "I couldn't think of a plan and you were taking a while, so . . ." He waved his arms around. "Here we are! Who's she?"

"She's Weed's —"

"I am Miss Josephine Du Monde and I am responsible for the cleanliness and sanctity of this 'ouse, which you, young man, 'ave just violated in a most severe way!"

"My bad," Mapper said, not looking very sorry.

The dactyl lifted one clawed foot then the other, its nails

scratching nasty gashes into the surface of Weed's once fancy desk, and squawked. "Uh," Mapper said, "isn't that what dactyls do right before they —" With a *ppffffttttt!* noise, the dactyl let loose a nasty, white-and-brown dropping directly onto the carpet. "— that."

"Oh my god," Magdalys said.

Miss Josephine shook her head. "Oh no no no no . . . no."

For a moment, they all just stared in disbelief. Then Miss Josephine very calmly walked over to the fireplace and picked up the matches again. She grabbed the basin of a hand lantern off the desk and turned it upside down, pouring oil all over the carpeted floor.

"What are you doing?" Magdalys yelled.

"What does it look like I am doing, filthy child? I am burning the place to the ground, oui?"

"But —"

"To be frank, I 'ave been dreaming of doing this for quite a few years now."

"But Mr. Weed . . ."

The dactyl screeched and took a few steps back from the noxious fumes now rising from the carpet. "Whoa," Mapper yelled.

"Mr. Weed," Josephine said, striking a match, "will beat me within an inch of my life if he finds the 'ouse in such a state."

Magdalys's eyes went wide. "Oh no . . ."

"If I am lucky. That's if he thinks eet was just from negligence that this 'appened, and not because I was spying. If eet's spying, he will 'ave me 'anged." The match didn't light, so she pulled out another.

"But I thought —"

"You thought slavery was abolished in New York?" Miss Josephine stopped what she was doing long enough to let out a sad, pitying belly laugh. "Okay, filthy child." She struck the second match. "But whatever silly thing you 'ave come to believe, you still better run."

"Wait!" Magdalys yelled. "The papers! The rest of them. They might . . . My family. Weed was the one who stashed me in the orphanage, and he took my sisters back to Cuba. I have to . . . I have to find out what I can."

Miss Josephine shook out the match. "Ah, you are one of the orphans . . . Of course. Very well, quickly now. All of his papers are in this cabinet 'ere." She nodded at a big wooden cabinet against the wall. "Grab what you can. I am setting this fire in two minutes. And I will have burnt up in the fire, of course, because after today New York will hear no more of Miss Josephine Du Monde, that I promise you."

"But you're not really going to let it burn you up, right?" Mapper said.

"Mapper!" Magdalys snapped. "Come help me with these papers!"

He hopped off the dactyl, careful not to land in the massive mound of pteropoop, and hurried over, satchel open. Together they shoved as many documents as they could fit in their bags as Miss Josephine watched approvingly. When they finished, she nodded at them, struck the match, and dropped it.

All three of them climbed on the dactyl as the flames roared to life behind them. "Go!" Mapper yelled. "Heeyah!" And the dactyl took off through the smashed window and soared out into the Manhattan skies.

CHAPTER TWENTY-THREE
HEDGEHOG, GRANTED

IT WAS JUST past noon by the time Magdalys, Mapper, and Miss Josephine made it back to the Bochinche. They stumbled in, exhausted and filthy from their long journey and near escape from the flames, the two satchels full of documents clutched tightly in their arms.

People packed the bar from wall to wall. Magdalys had never seen it so full. They squeezed in and closed the door behind them. "What's going on?" Mapper asked, and someone promptly shushed him.

"It's about to start!" a voice from up front called.

"Ooh, a play!" Miss Josephine, who could see over everyone's heads, exclaimed.

A play? Magdalys got on tippy-toes but still couldn't see what was happening. Then everyone started roaring and clapping and she heard Halsey Crunk proclaim: "Now is the winter of our discontent!"

"I know that's right," a woman in the audience shouted, and everyone cackled. Some other performer might've been thrown by the hootenanny, but Magdalys knew Halsey; she'd seen him perform at least a dozen times, and he lived for exactly that lively, loving audience interaction that was happening in the Bochinche. He was probably frowning, deep in character as Richard III, the conniving, hunchbacked king of England, but inside, Halsey was chuckling away.

"Made glorious summer by this son of *New* York!"

That *New* definitely wasn't in the original play. Even if you didn't know, it was obvious by the way Halsey threw it in, and either way, the audience *loved* him for it. Raucous laughter broke out followed by wild applause.

Halsey went on, seemingly oblivious, and for a few moments, Magdalys lost herself in the tumbling speech, its highs and lows and wishes and fears. She let the words take her away to some world where things didn't keep catching fire around her and death didn't lurk around every corner. Then again, *Richard III* was one of Shakespeare's bloodiest plays — she would always remember the soggy paper bags with something heavy in it that they'd used to show proof of some beheaded dukes at the Zanzibar, and the chills it gave her.

The nagging weight on her shoulder brought Magdalys back to reality. Riker and Weed were shipping those orphans out of New York tonight. She had to let David and Cymbeline know.

Magdalys poked Mapper, who stood completely enthralled by the play even though he couldn't see either. He looked up like he'd been shaken out of a deep sleep, and she motioned for him to pass her the satchel. Then she made her way through the crowd.

"Dost grant me, hedgehog?" Cymbeline's voice sang out from the stage. The audience hollered. "Then god grant me too: Thou mayst be damned for that wicked deed!"

David was nowhere to be seen, but Bernice was behind the bar, drying beer mugs and shooting dirty looks at anybody who got out of line. She flashed a big smile when Magdalys finally made it over to her. "Hey, babygirl!" she whispered. "I've always wanted to turn this place into a theater on top of everything else. And now look! How was Manhattan?"

Magdalys didn't even know where to start. "I need to talk to Mr. Ballantine. I . . . I have something for him. Is he here? It's important."

"No, dear, but he should be back soon. Said Mr. Napoleon sent a dactyl bout something urgent and he had to rush off."

Magdalys gulped. Had the fire stirred up some other trouble for the Vigilance Committee? What if everyone had been arrested or snatched up?

"You look scared and tired, dearie, and you're filthy! Goodness. Why don't you go bathe. I'll set some dinner out for you in the back room and you can wait for Mr. Ballantine there."

Magdalys nodded. The sheer exhaustion of the day felt like a weight that dragged her toward the ground with each passing moment. "Can you let him know . . ." she mumbled, ". . . it's important?"

"Of course, love," Bernice said, ushering her toward the stairs. "I'll tell him when I see him."

Magdalys woke with a start. The sun was just beginning its long summer afternoon journey toward the Manhattan building tops.

The satchels.

She peered under the bed, gaped at the dusty emptiness. She'd stashed them under there while she bathed and dressed herself with every intention of going downstairs to wait for Mr. Ballantine, and then promptly passed all the way out instead.

How long had she slept? She had no idea. More importantly: *Where were the satchels?* All that information, even if it made no sense at all to her yet, had to matter. It had to! After all they'd gone through to get it. But there was nothing under the bed. Nothing under any of the beds. Nothing behind the cabinets or in the one closet or beneath the window drapes. Nothing. The satchels were gone.

Had Miss Bernice stolen them? Had she been deceiving them all this time? Magdalys bolted out of the room and down the dark stairwell. The bar was emptying out, the show having just ended. Bernice was nowhere to be seen; Mr. Barrett was behind the bar as usual. Magdalys glanced frantically around, then dashed to the back room and stopped short in the doorway.

"That's gotta mean Rio de Janeiro," Amaya was saying. "Where's that at?"

"Brazil," Mapper said, without missing a beat.

"What about this one?" Amaya crossed the floor with a piece of paper in her hand. A soot-covered piece of paper. The wall behind them was covered, floor to ceiling, in Harrison Weed's stolen documents. That circular seal with the tyrannosaurus glared out from almost every sheet of paper. Magdalys burst out laughing.

"Oh, hey, Mag-D!" Two Step called from his perch at the top of a ladder. She hadn't even seen him up there. "We were just trying to make sense of those papers you and Mapper ganked this morning." He glanced at the paper Amaya had handed up to him. "Oh, that goes over in stack number one, I think. Nicaragua."

"Anyway," Mapper said, "seems ol' boy is involved pretty deeply in some kind of international trade. He's got documents and ledgers detailing sales from here all through the Confederate states, Cuba, and throughout South America."

"Sales of what?" Magdalys asked, though she was pretty sure she already knew the answer.

Mapper looked at the others, then back at Magdalys. "Uh . . . us."

She nodded, sat down. Even knowing it already hadn't softened the blow. The staggering cruelty of the human race seemed to sink into her blood and bones. It wasn't the first time; she knew it wouldn't be the last. She shook her head, letting it all spin around her for a terrible few moments. All those numbers now decorating the walls, those were all people, somehow. Even if they were dollar amounts or cargo numbers, one way or another they all traced back to human beings. One of them was probably about her. And another her brother and sisters.

"Pretty sure I cracked the code though," Mapper said. "At least the basics of it."

Code! Magdalys dug through her pockets, pulled out the scrap of paper she'd found. "Guys," she said, placing it on the table and unfolding it carefully. They gathered around and read.

"The others . . ." Amaya said, fists tight, brow furrowed.

"We gotta . . . We have to . . ." Two Step said.

"We will," Amaya said. "We will."

CHAPTER TWENTY-FOUR

TROUBLE AND MORE TROUBLE

IT WAS WELL past five o'clock when David, Cymbeline, and Louis Napoleon walked through the door of the back room arm in arm like they'd been friends their whole lives. David stopped mid-laughter when he saw Magdalys, Mapper, Two Step, and Amaya gathered around the stack of papers on the big wooden table. (Sabeen had long since curled up and passed out in the corner.)

"Magdalys Roca," David said, smile gone. "I just spoke with a certain Miss Josephine —"

Magdalys held up a hand. "I know what you're going to say, Mr. Ballantine, and I'm sorry I disobeyed a direct order, but —"

"I don't think you do, Magdalys." David's voice was ice. "And I don't care what the but is; we can talk about that later."

Magdalys sat. All the stern talking-tos she'd gotten at the orphanage, all the wagging fingers and tight faces . . . they circled back around her like a whirlwind of shame. This was different, she knew this was different, but still . . . the echoes remained.

"When I give an order," David said, crossing his arms over his chest, "it's not because I'm power tripping or just trying to boss you around. I'm doing it because I don't want you to die." His voice cracked a little, and Magdalys was suddenly terrified he was going to burst into tears. "There's so much happening right now, so much danger. For all of us. And you going off on your own, or even dragging someone else along with you on some wild mission to do who knows what —"

"We were —" Mapper started, but David cut him off with a single glare.

"And it's not just Miss Josephine."

Magdalys looked up from her hands.

"Old Wilco Badhoffer came to the Bochinche earlier to complain that some of the chimney sweeps had flown on dactyl-back to the bone factory on the edge of town."

"What's a bone factory?" Mapper asked.

"The silo out by those cow pastures that I'm quite positive Miss Bernice told you not to go anywhere near. They slaughter those cows, sell off the meat to places like the Bochinche, and then grind up the bones to make fertilizer."

"But . . . how?"

"That's what I'm getting to. They say that's how Dactyl

Hill got its name — all that carrion attracted the pteros, and here we are. Badhoffer was upset because whoever was there got his pteranodon all riled up."

Magdalys's eyes went wide. There was a pteranodon in the silo? A pteranodon was like a pterodactyl but way, waaay bigger and with no teeth and not much of a tail. Dr. Barlow Sloan's Dinoguide said they were the most intelligent and graceful of the pteros, and fiercely protective of their brood. And if the creature in that silo was one, it was even more gigantic than the average pteranodon.

Two Step boggled. "That thing was a pteranodon? Whoa!"

Cymbeline shook her head. "You kids are terrible at keeping secrets."

"Thanks for the confession, Two Step," David said. "And I imagine Magdalys was with you?"

Two Step crossed an imaginary zipper over his lips. Everyone stared at Magdalys; she just looked away, face sullen. It didn't even matter if she got caught anymore. The pteranodon changed everything.

"You guys don't have legal guardians right now," David said. "And we figured, quite frankly, between myself, Louis, the Crunks — well, Cymbeline, at least — Bernice, and everyone else here, we'd do a better job of keeping you guys safe than the broken ol' charity bureaucracy. But now . . . if you won't even follow simple orders, I'm not so sure."

Magdalys felt the blood pounding through her face. Being back in an orphanage would be like prison. There would be no way out, no way to get south. Her whole body pulsed with the need to grab her things and be gone, grab her things and be gone. But she wouldn't give anyone the satisfaction of seeing her storm away.

"I don't like holding that over your heads," David said, "but I don't know how else to get through to you that this is life and death for us all."

Magdalys had had enough. She stood, rustled around in her pocket, then pulled Riker's note back out and put it on the table. David picked it up. Cymbeline and Louis looked over his shoulder. David read it out loud to Louis.

"Did . . ." Louis said.

"Do . . ." Cymbeline said.

"But . . ." David said.

All three shook their heads. "Eleven tonight," David finally managed. "That gives us a couple hours . . ."

"It corroborates what Marietta and I found out earlier," Louis said. "That all but forty-five of the orphans are accounted for by the Anti-Slavery Society."

David nodded, his eyes far away. "Louis, get the —"

Louis Napoleon was already halfway out the door. "On it."

"We need to make moves and we need to do it fast," David said. "Meet back here in an hour."

Magdalys turned around and walked away from the table.

"Magdalys," David called. "I'm not through talking to you."

"Give her a minute," Cymbeline said quietly.

"Meet back here?" Mapper gaped. "So we can —"

“So you can tell me what plan you’ve come up with,” David said grimly.

The Dactyl Hill Squad let a single second of silence past before jumping into action. “Mapper,” Two Step said, “let’s get mapping!”

“Yes, sir!” Mapper called back. Amaya followed him as he started gathering papers.

Magdalys walked out of the room and closed the door behind her.

“Save it,” Magdalys said when Two Step appeared in the doorway. She’d just finished packing her satchel and she wasn’t interested.

“What are you doing, Mag-D?”

She shook her head. “And people say *I* don’t listen.” She brushed past him, holding back tears, and headed down the hallway.

“Magdalys, you can’t just leave!”

She spun around, barely breathing. “Watch me.”

CHAPTER TWENTY-FIVE
SILO JONES

IT FELT GOOD, this clarity, and it felt terrible.

A fierce wind flushed against Magdalys's face as she guided her dactyl in reckless dips through the purple-and-orange clouds. Far below, cows speckled the rolling pastures, their shadows stretching toward the silo.

She knew what she had to do. For the first time since finding out Montez was wounded, Magdalys knew what to do. The dactyl panted beneath her. She could feel its exhaustion in her own weary muscles, that heaviness a relentless clucking fuss in her mind. But she was so close.

"Wait!" Two Step's voice came to her over the rushing wind. She shook her head, glancing back with a frown. Kid didn't know when to quit. And even though his dactyl was swooping wildly through the clouds, they weren't far back.

"Mr. Ballantine just told you not to come near this place!" Two Step yelled.

"Yep."

"And here you are."

Magdalys didn't bother answering.

The dactyls swooped and spiraled above the bone factory en masse, just like before, and she and Two Step had to do some fancy flying to avoid collisions as they came in for rocky landings on the edge of the wall.

The stench, growing at a steady pace as they approached, rose up suddenly to greet them like an excited puppy. And then: *Yeeeeeeeoooooooorrrrrrrrrmmmmmghhh!!!!*

"I know," Magdalys whispered. "I'm here." It almost sounded like it recognized her; like it was maybe glad she'd come back to visit again. Could that be?

Ooooooooooooooghhhhrrrraaaaaahh!!! But the sorrow was still so palpable; she could almost taste it.

The beast wanted freedom. It wanted to . . . She closed her eyes, ignored the rumble of nervousness she had about leaving, her cycling spiral of worry about the kidnapped orphans, the fierce nudge of Two Step's anxiety, and her own guilt. She let the world fall away for a moment and then she saw it: wide-open skies. Clouds zooming past. The setting sun on one side and rising moon on the other. The whole world from above. Freedom.

Magdalys turned to the dark, stench-filled pit below and whispered, "It's time."

"Mags," Two Step said. "Okay, I get that you *can* leave, but . . . don't? Please?"

Magdalys just stared at him. She didn't have any words, so there was no sense in speaking.

"We . . ." Two Step ran a hand over his fro. "We need you, Magdalys. The other kids need you. All of us do. *I* need you."

Something inside Magdalys felt like it was tearing in half. Was this what Montez had felt? Why he'd run off to fight a war in a whole other part of the country? Of course Magdalys wanted to stay. And of course she wanted to go. She'd never been needed before; at least, she'd never felt that way. But Montez needed her too. Or she needed him. She needed him to be okay. And this was the best way to make sure of that. The only way.

She looked Two Step in his eyes. "Come with me."

For a second, he just stood there, a tear worrying the edge of his eye, and she thought maybe he'd say yes. A gentle rain splattered the silo and played tiny pings against the tin roof. Two Step shook his head. "I can't." He turned around, walked back to his dactyl, and took off.

"Tell them I'm sorry," Magdalys said, but she didn't know if he heard her over the wind.

The chains fell away pretty easily with a little help from the hatchet Magdalys had borrowed from the Bochinche's storage room. And then all that was left was that tin roof, halfway covering the gaping entrance of the silo. In the darkness beneath it, something huge stirred, grunted, and then growled. The rain started falling in earnest as Magdalys heaved it aside with a clang.

"Hey, girl," Magdalys said. A huge head emerged from the shadows, and Magdalys could make out some of the wings and body. Majestic as she was, the poor creature's skin looked too pale and sickly. Old scars and some festering blisters stretched along her hide. A few of her claws were chipped, and Magdalys could count the ribs running along her torso.

Eeeeyoo? The pteranodon seemed to be posing a question for her, but Magdalys had no idea what it was.

"Magdalys!" she yelled. "That's my name. And I'll call you . . . Stella!"

Roooooooagggbh! Stella howled, and it felt like a yes.

"Yes, girl," Magdalys said. "You're free now. Come on through."

The pteranodon was even bigger than Magdalys had thought she would be.

Way bigger.

Magdalys's mouth fell open as the humongous beak surged out of the silo, followed by the head. And then more of the head, then the long bony crest stretching back over the wide neck. And finally, what felt like a full couple of minutes later, the pteranodon's torso and giant wings.

Magdalys crouched, preparing to jump. If she timed it

right, she should be able to grab onto her arched back and hold tight, and then the wind would whip through her hair and they'd be off and away. Free.

Magdalys steadied herself, legs trembling with anticipation. Not yet. The huge beast kept on going. Almost. The torso narrowed to a long, long tail.

Magdalys watched her pass. At some point, she'd stopped crouching. Now she was just sitting.

Arrrrrroooooooooooooooooooooooogghhhh!! the pteranodon howled in Magdalys's mind, and it sounded something like joy. The joy of sudden freedom after being kept for so long in that dank hole.

Magdalys remembered the recoil she'd felt just a little while ago when David had mentioned going back into the orphanage's custody. She wondered what the pteranodon had been through, what she felt like, tasting the sky for the first time in so long after only seeing glimpses of it. To be so huge and trapped by such tiny, useless creatures.

Dactyls scattered to either side as Stella exploded into the air above the silo. Magdalys's mouth dropped open. The pteranodon was bigger than enormous. Magdalys could still beckon her, demand a ride, or at least ask for one. Maybe the huge ptero would listen. Instead, Magdalys sat, letting the rain cascade down on her.

Stella swooped a long, joyous circle, hooting her thanks and excitement, and then took off into the cloud-strewn skies.

For a long time, Magdalys watched her fly.

CHAPTER TWENTY-SIX

PLOTTING & PLANNING, PLANNING & PLOTTING

BY THE TIME Magdalys stepped back into the Bochinche, she was soaked to the bone, but she felt like a tiny weight had lifted off her heart. She wouldn't be able to go find Montez just yet, and accepting that truth was as freeing as it was sad. She had to let go of that dream, at least for now, and concentrate on the people closer to home who needed her help.

"Mag-D!" Two Step yelled, bolting across the bar and embracing her. "You came back," he whispered. "I knew you would!"

"No you didn't," Magdalys said, but she was smiling. That hushed tone meant he hadn't told the others that she'd been about to abandon them. "*I* didn't even know I'd come back." She hugged him back and squeezed with all her might.

"Why you soakin' wet, Mags?" Mapper yelled from a table in the corner. "Come help me draw up these secret plans!"

Magdalys shook her head, still smiling, as Two Step broke into a wild dance and Sabeen came over to see what the commotion was. "You okay?" she asked, gazing up at Magdalys. "I saw Two Step leave after you and I got worried."

"I wasn't," Magdalys said, hugging Sabeen. "But I am now. Kinda."

"It's time!" David called from the backroom door. "Squad report!"

"Oh boy!" Mapper said, rolling up his papers and hopping down from the table.

Magdalys shook her head. "Let me change out of these wet clothes so I can see what wildness you guys came up with."

"Now, what you got?" David said. He and Louis Napoleon pulled up chairs, spun them around, and sat backward in them. Miss Josephine and Cymbeline sat on either side of them, and all four were gazing at the complicated mess of arrows and pictures that Mapper, Two Step, Amaya, and Sabeen had scribbled over the map. Cymbeline leaned over the table like a master strategist, face scrunched up. "Looks like that time David tried to write a novel," Louis snickered.

"Hush, you," David snapped.

Mapper stood and cleared his throat. "Alright, here it is.

We figure the *Ocarrion* is docked in New York Harbor, right? And they'll probably have a gang of Kidnapping Club goons out and about for security on the docks, yeah? So we dactylride rooftop to rooftop down to the water, then we each hide out in one of the docked boats, and when the *Ocarrion* heads out to sea, we swoop in after 'em and take it over, kick all the slavers over the side and commandeer it back to the bay and turn the orphans back over to the Anti-Slavery Society and boom! Mission accomplished."

As all five kids waited with eager eyes, Louis and David exchanged a look, then returned their gaze to Mapper.

"That's not bad," David said. "Not bad at all."

"I sense a big but coming," Amaya said.

Mapper snickered.

"Not that kind of butt!" she snapped.

"Look," Louis said. "David and I are going to tear your plan apart, but not because it's not a good plan. Because that's what we do in the Vigilance Committee when one of us makes a plan."

"You shred it?" Two Step asked.

"I mean, kinda," David said. "But not in a mean way. It means we're taking you seriously. Means you're one of us." Magdalys felt a little burst of warmth in her chest — *one of us*. She was glad she'd come back. "And we do it," David continued, "because we know that during an operation, everything that might go wrong will."

"Plus about five hundred other things you didn't expect to," Cymbeline added.

"Exactly," David said. "And why Miss Cymbeline here knows so much about handling firearms *and* conducting covert ops will apparently remain a secret."

Cymbeline smiled in a self-satisfied kind of way. "I am but a humble actress, sir!"

"Will remain a secret *for now*," David added sharply. "In the meantime, you can help us shred the youngens' plan, as Two Step so aptly put it."

"Good," Cymbeline said. "I'll start then. What if the boat isn't in the harbor?"

"Then it's either already left," Amaya said.

"Or?"

"Or it's leaving from somewhere else," Magdalys said.

"Or?"

"Or it's not leaving at all, the note was wrong, or they changed plans," Two Step said.

"Good," David and Cymbeline said at the same time.

"So we put a guy on Riker and a guy on this Weed dude," Mapper said. "And the guys —"

"Or girls," Amaya put in.

"Or girls, or whatever, send word via minidact about their movements."

"Excellent," Louis said, eyebrows raised, grin wide. "We already did that. Haven't located Magistrate Riker yet, but Mr. Harrison Weed is currently busy having what was left of his stuff moved to a nearby apartment."

Two Step high-fived Magdalys and Mapper. "It wasn't us,"

Magdalys pointed out. "Credit where it's due. Miss Josephine really made that happen."

"De rien," Miss Josephine said.

"It's all well and good that we inconvenienced that maniac," David said, "but the real haul from Magdalys and Mapper's little Manhattan sojourn is the paperwork." He gestured to the vast collage of documents pinned to the walls around them. "We've long suspected there was coordination amongst the international slavers in Havana and Rio and the New York pro-slavery forces. It's called the Golden Circle, and it spans locations all across Central and South America and the Caribbean. Now it looks like we — or should I say, you all — have uncovered one of the key linchpins in that connection. Harrison Weed, who we now know is a member of a secret society called the Knights of the Golden Circle —"

"K of the G C!" Magdalys blurted out. Everyone looked at her. "The seal that's all over Weed's paperwork! And Riker's medallion!"

"Exactly," David said. "Weed has been communicating with shipping companies and other 'knights,' plantation masters and politicians mostly, all throughout the Americas. Including Riker, whose Kidnapper Club is basically a local offshoot of the Golden Circle. And it's pretty clear that the cargo they're all discussing is . . . human."

Magdalys shuddered. She'd known it, but still, hearing it said out loud again brought a sick feeling inside her. All those people, shoved into the bellies of ships and left to die . . . If

Weed was coordinating with slavers, and he'd brought her and her family to New York, did that mean . . .

"More than that," David continued, "you've drawn a direct line connecting him to the one and only City Magistrate Richard Riker, head of the Kidnapping Club. You should be proud of yourselves."

General congratulating and hooting ensued. David cut it short: "But! But. What that means is, both Riker and Weed probably suspect someone's onto them, and they probably suspect that someone is us."

"They're gonna have to prove it," Mapper said.

Louis Napoleon stood up and shook his head. "Ah, but they're not. They've never bothered proving anything before — that's what makes them so dangerous. With an officer of the city involved, they make the law do whatever it wants for them."

"They certainly haven't needed any proof to send our folks down south in chains over and over," David said. "And they won't be waiting for proof now either. That means we all have to be extra, extra on guard and ready for anything."

Everyone nodded. Magdalys noticed Two Step and Mapper had spun their chairs around and straddled them backward the way David and Louis did. She smiled inwardly. It was good to see the boys had some role models. And she was pretty sure she wanted to be exactly like Cymbeline when she grew up, except for the acting part.

"*Anything*," Cymbeline added, standing. "So the mission is

this: Find the *Ocarrion*, and seize it. If the kidnapped orphans are already on board, we free 'em and commandeer the *Ocarrion* back to port." Magdalys noticed David nodding. "If they're not, we lay in wait, catch whoever's bringing them red-handed, and bring them down to the courthouse, after freeing the orphans. We stay in touch via messenger dactyl. Any questions?"

Magdalys raised her hand. "What's going to happen to Miss Josephine?"

Miss Josephine chuckled. "Oh, I will be alright, mon cherie. Monsieur Ballantine has arranged safe passage for me on a ship bound for Haiti tomorrow." Magdalys loved how Miss Josephine pronounced the name of her homeland: *Ayee-tee*. On the way back from Manhattan, she'd regaled them with tales of her life in Paris, where she'd been educated, and the few memories she had of being a young girl in Port-au-Prince. Magdalys had read stories about Haiti in the papers: a free black state. One day she hoped to visit.

"Point number two," Cymbeline said. "What if the *Ocarrion* is there, but it's fast, makes it out to sea before we can catch up?"

"Or what if the dactyls get tired and can't make it all the way out to wherever it is?" Louis added.

Magdalys opened her mouth but then realized she had nothing to respond with. Neither, it seemed, did anyone else.

David laughed. "That's why it's a good thing the Vigilance Committee has access to a mosasaurus."

Everyone, including Cymbeline and Louis, gaped at him.

Some people didn't even believe the mosasaurs existed, certainly not anywhere near New York City. They weren't even technically dinos, as if the creatures were so huge and ridiculous they needed their own entire type of monstrosity to encompass them. And the mosasaurus — that was the biggest, meanest, toothiest, most unstoppable mosasaur there was. Magdalys was rendered speechless.

"We do?" Louis said.

"Yeah." David's brow furrowed. "Now if only we knew someone who could ride it . . ."

Everyone looked at Magdalys.

PART THREE

RESCUE RUN

CHAPTER TWENTY-SEVEN

OUT AND AWAY OVER THE ROOFTOPS

"I DON'T LIKE IT," David said for the fifty-thousandth time since it had been decided.

Everyone groaned. They were in a top-secret, even further back back room of the Bochinche, loading all kinds of fierce weapons into shoulder bags.

At first he'd outright refused the entire idea of Magdalys piloting the mosasaurus. The others had protested and begged on her behalf, even Cymbeline, and it had finally taken a demonstration of her skills to bring him around: Magdalys had called a medium-sized dactyl to her, sent him spiraling in a wild loop-de-loop through the sky, and then had him snatch Louis Napoleon's cap right off his head before landing back on her wrist with barely a squawk.

Not even a professional dinowrangler could've pulled that off, and everyone knew it. Magdalys had something special going for her. She didn't even try to explain the strange sounds she heard inside herself or how they somehow made sense to her, all those moans and grunts giving voice to emotions like they were speaking in perfectly clear English. Why bother? It was enough for them to know that she could do it, could get the dinos to do as she asked without so much as meeting them first, let alone training them for months like a dinowrangler would've had to do. And anyway, Magdalys was still pretty sure no one would believe her. They'd probably think she was nuts.

"She's like the dinoriding warriors of old," Bernice had whispered. "Never seen anything like it."

David had finally relented, begrudgingly, and that meant that the rest of the squad was going as well.

And now they were finishing the last bits of prep and David stood across from them, cleaning his pistol and looking as surly as Magdalys had ever seen him.

"I just . . . I don't like it," David said again.

"We know," Sabeen said. "You keep telling us."

"One thing we've all been wondering though," Mapper said, "is do you like it?"

David grumbled something indecipherable and probably rude and holstered his pistol.

"We'll be careful," Magdalys said. "We promise. And if anything happens, it's on us, not you."

"Ha," David snorted. "Easy for you to say. I'll be the one who has to live with myself if you get hurt, or . . . worse."

Everyone got quiet at that. They knew death was a possibility, but the mention of it still felt better left unsaid, even when it was left unsaid.

Louis Napoleon poked his head in. "It's time."

Everyone climbed up to the roof of the Bochinche together. The rain had cleared and now the sun was sliding into a towering mountain of clouds over Dactyl Hill. Down below, Brooklyn grew taller and denser as it sloped toward the river. Sauropod necks loomed over the rowhouses, carrying commuters back home after a long day grinding in Manhattan.

Magdalys took a deep breath. This was the last time they'd be together as a group before attacking the *Ocarrion*. She tried not to think about all the what-ifs, but they crowded in anyway: gruesome, haunting images of her own death and that of all her friends. And then those other thoughts returned, an ever-lingering, uninvited phantom at her door. Why should she and her friends make it anyway? So many others hadn't. So many had been killed; so many more would die. And she'd almost left them all behind. What right did Magdalys have to be alive?

Cymbeline's hand landed on her shoulder, bringing her back to the world. "I'm proud of you, Magdalys."

"Why?" Magdalys said, trying and failing to keep the bitterness from her voice. "I haven't really done anything yet."

Cymbeline rolled her eyes, but she was smiling. "You survived, Magdalys. Not just your body but your soul too. I see how you look out for the others, how you love them and they love you. It's no small thing. It's maybe the biggest thing. I know that might not make sense now, but trust me. You being alive is the answer to a great many prayers."

Magdalys didn't know what to say, so she just hugged Cymbeline as hard as she could.

They gathered in a circle. "You already know I need you each to make it out of this okay," David said, "for purely selfish reasons. If you get hurt, I'll never forgive you." He locked eyes with each of them. "The Dactyl Hill Squad." He shook his head. "You guys are alright. Now, we regroup at the harbor in one hour," David said. "So we better get moving. Everyone's to travel in pairs and take up your positions as instructed. Magdalys, you and Amaya are linking with an operative named Redd at Pier 54. You can trust him and his cutlass entirely — he's one of our best."

Magdalys raised her eyebrows. *Cutlass?*

"YAAA!!" Mapper yelled after David gave everyone else their assignments. Their hands all met in the middle and a great hurrah went up.

Then, two by two, the Dactyl Hill Squad hopped on dactylback and swooped out into the sky over Brooklyn.

CHAPTER TWENTY-EIGHT
PIERS & PIRATES

MAGDALYS AND AMAYA went through three dactyls on the journey; once they'd crossed over from Brooklyn they still had to trek to the other end of Manhattan, and the whole time the harried city streets seemed ready to swallow them whole at any moment.

Finally, they found it, came in for a rocky landing, and released their steeds. Up ahead, Pier 54 stretched out from a series of warehouses and dilapidated shacks over the Hudson River. The dark shores of New Jersey seemed to glare at them from the other side. A sauropod ferry passed, heading south toward the bay, crates trailing along on a barge behind it.

"See anyone?" Magdalys asked. Amaya shook her head. Glancing from side to side, they walked toward the gloomy shipyard. "Do we just — ?"

Footsteps raced toward them, but Magdalys couldn't tell where from. Amaya was already loading black powder into the pistol Cymbeline had given her.

"Ay!" someone called from behind them. Magdalys and Amaya whirled around. A tall boy sprinted around a corner toward them. He did something with his hands and Magdalys flinched back a step; Amaya cocked her raised pistol. A minidactyl fluttered up out of the boy's grasp and then shot off into the sky, a tiny roll of paper clutched in its claws.

Magdalys relaxed a tiny bit. This had to be Redd, right? She made the *V* and *C* signs on her chest as he ran up to them, but he didn't stop, just laughed and ran past, then stopped a few paces on when he realized they weren't following.

"You comin'?" The boy had high cheekbones and freckles and light brown skin lit up by the setting sun, which cast a long dancing shadow onto the causeway behind him. He'd had a thin goatee line tattooed along the edge of his jaw. A loose, raggedy shirt hung from his slender shoulders, and white cloth wrapped around his chest beneath it.

That cutlass David had mentioned hung from one of the belts crisscrossing his waist; a pistol was holstered in the other. He finally looked down at Magdalys's hand signs. "Oh yeah, VC, VC, I know! I'm Redd. You all are Magdalys and Amaya. I got the description. And sorry to rush you and cut through the formalities 'n' whatnot, but we gotta roll!"

Magdalys and Amaya exchanged a look, then fell into a fast walk behind him as he took off toward the pier again.

"Just got a dactyl from David," Redd said. "Here, you can read it. Just read while you run." He handed back a crumpled scrap of parchment, slowing down only slightly so Magdalys could grab it.

We lost track of R.
Weed stayed put but his men made for the harbor, boarded a small rowboat.
We think exchange happened earlier — orphans already on boat.
In pursuit.
Either the O is docked out in the harbor islands somewhere or mission is aborted.
Ride out with M and A and rendezvous at the Spine Islands.

"Toss it when you done," Redd said, guiding them through a labyrinth of shipping crates and ironworks. Magdalys passed Amaya the note, who read it and then tore it into little pieces that fluttered away on the early evening breeze.

"There she is," Redd said, finally stopping at the edge of the pier, arms akimbo like a proud father. "They say you're the only wrangler who can handle her."

In all the excitement, Magdalys hadn't had time to think about how she was about to ride one of the most dangerous and unmanageable creatures in the modern world. And that many lives depended on her not messing it up, including her own. And she had no idea what she was doing, not really.

She stared into the waves lapping up against the pier, their edges bright with the sinking July sun. A huge, dark shape lurked just below the surface. It had to be sixty feet, at least. The mosasaurus was wide in the middle, where a worn leather saddle breached the water. Her long, black-and-yellow striated body narrowed some toward the head and even more at the tail, which swished slowly back and forth in what seemed like murderous anticipation. Huge fins on either side splashed at the surface of the water.

"Ready?" Redd asked, already halfway down the wooden ladder. "Nobody's really been able to figure out how to ride her, to be honest. A couple of my men have tried though."

"Yep," Magdalys said, trying to look confident. "Go 'head, Amaya, I'll go after you."

Amaya eyed her, obviously seeing right through her as always, then squeezed her shoulder one time, holstered the pistol, and climbed down after Redd. "Your men?" Amaya asked once she'd lowered herself onto the saddle behind Redd.

"Yeah, I'm only contracting with the Vigilance Committee now and then. Got my own crew, really. We buccaneers."

"You mean pirates?" Amaya said.

Redd chuckled. "Pretty much. Riding the deep sea, tracking slave ships and boarding 'em, freein' everybody. That kinda thing."

Magdalys barely heard them. It was one thing to boast to

David about her ease with dinowrangling. She had the whole squad with her doing most of the boasting anyway, and Cymbeline sealed the deal. Then sending that dactyl up into the air had been a piece of cake really. But now, it all seemed so impossible. The burden of all that responsibility loomed over her.

"You comin', sis?" Redd called. "We don't have much time."

She took a deep breath. She could do this.

What if the beast didn't respond to her? What if she ate Magdalys and everyone else? Or took them out to the deep sea and drowned them? What if the Ocarrion *blew them out of the water?*

Deep breath.

She could do this. She nodded once, more to herself than Redd, then climbed down the ladder just as a horrendous roar erupted from the water.

CHAPTER TWENTY-NINE
OUT INTO THE BLUE

"WHOA, MISSY, WHOA," Redd yelled.

Magdalys sped down the ladder and leapt onto the front end of the mosasaurus's damp saddle. The beast thrashed and snarled.

Easy, Magdalys thought. *Shhhh.*

The reply came as a violent, desperate howling inside her. This was a whole other caliber of monster, Magdalys realized. In the Dinoguide, Dr. Barlow Sloan described mosasauruses as *extraordinarily ferocious, almost entirely untrainable. Nearly every attempt to domesticate a mosasaurus,* he went on, somewhat rudely Magdalys now thought, *has ended in dismemberment and death. And not for the mosasaurus, if you catch our meaning. For the trainer, just to be clear.*

And this particular mosasaurus was hungry. Magdalys felt Missy's frantic urge to hunt pulse through her, relentless.

We're going, Missy, we're going, I promise. Just . . . easy . . . easy.

The mosasaurus kept thrashing, sending foamy waves to either side. "Cut the line," Magdalys said. She grabbed the reins. "We out."

"Ay, ay, Captain," Redd called, unsheathing his cutlass and slicing away the rope with a yelp. "And away!"

The mosasaurus didn't have to be told twice. They hurtled forward with such a violent lurch that all three almost toppled into the Hudson.

Easy! Magdalys commanded, throwing some growl into her thoughts this time.

Missy seemed to hear her. The sea monster fell into a smooth glide just below the surface, the dark water skimming to either side as they flushed along the river toward the bay.

"Not bad!" Redd yelled from the back.

Magdalys turned and shot him a smile just in time to almost get thrown again as Missy cut a sudden right and nearly barrel-rolled underwater. "Whoa!" Magdalys yelled. "I said, easy, Missy!"

The mosasaurus slid back into her smooth glide and Magdalys shook her head. This wasn't going to be easy.

"The Spine Islands that way," Redd said as they hurtled on a rambunctious charge into the harbor. He pointed out toward some black shapes rising from the water against the darkening horizon, then raised a spyglass. "I don't see no one out there, but let's go anyway, see what we find."

A dactyl zipped by overhead, but it didn't look like it was carrying any messages.

Magdalys pulled the reins toward the islands and Missy growled in response, and then surged in the opposite direction before spinning back around and blasting forward full speed.

"You good?" Amaya asked from behind her.

"Yeah," Magdalys said. "Pretty sure Missy is doing her best to mess with me in every possible way. But I got her." The mosasaurus grunted and arched her back, sliding beneath the water just enough to soak all three of their boots before launching back up and lifting above the crashing waves, then slamming down with a gigantic splash.

"Whoosah!" Magdalys yelled as the smell of salt water reached her on the ocean wind.

But where were the others? And where was the *Ocarrion*?

She scanned the water stretching out all around as they approached the islands. Nothing. Behind them, New York City seemed to rise out of the sea, but it didn't look so tall and imposing from out here, more like a toy set. For a few moments, all they heard were the lapping of waves and occasional grunts and snorts from Missy, her snout resting just at the top of the water. Redd passed Amaya a carbine out of his satchel and then raised his spyglass again as she prepped it.

"There!" Redd yelled. "A ship." He passed Magdalys the telescope.

The world just looked like a blurry mess of shadows for a few moments while she adjusted her eyes. Then she saw it, way off in the waves: a medium-sized steam frigate, its long masts reaching up into the night and beneath them a squat chimney. "The *Ocarrion*?" she asked.

"Guessin' so," Redd said just as the crack of a musket sounded in the distance. "And not a moment too soon — something's happenin'!"

"Heeyah!" Magdalys yelled, and Missy launched forward like she'd been waiting her whole life to charge an iron-sided slave-trading steamship.

CHAPTER THIRTY
BATTLE FOR THE *OCARRION*

AS THEY SPED toward the frigate, Magdalys started making out shapes in the sky above it. Dactyls! The squad had reached the *Ocarrion*, or some of them had anyway. More gunfire erupted, and then the deeper blasts of artillery shells.

Faster! Magdalys urged, and Missy growled and blasted forward. Up ahead, a dactylrider nose-dived toward the *Ocarrion* deck. Magdalys heard screams and saw bright flashes as more musket shots rang out. She held her breath for a few seconds, then the dactyl swooped up from the other side, now riderless. More dactyls dove now, and shouts, squawks, and sword clangs rang out over the crashing waves.

"Uh, Magdalys," Redd called from behind her. "What are we going to do when we reach?"

Magdalys had just been wondering the exact same thing now that they were closing rapidly. She wasn't sure what the mosasaurus was capable of, though she'd heard of them being used to ram warships during the naval blockades down south. But the Dactyl Hill Squad and the Vigilance Committee were on board now, and she didn't know how many people she could safely fit on board Missy to bring them back to safety.

And anyway, it might not matter what Magdalys had planned at all. Missy let out a tremendous roar as they sped toward the ship. Her gigantic head rose out of the water, jaws spreading, and everything around them seemed to tremble, like Missy herself was a singular aquatic earthquake made of flesh, blood, tooth, and bone, and utterly unstoppable.

Magdalys lowered herself so her face was against Missy's cool hide. *Gently, mama, gently,* she cooed. Missy didn't seem to hear, just kept charging. *Just snatch 'em up easy, love. We don't want to destroy the whole boat. Please.*

She was pretty sure destroying the whole boat was *exactly* what Missy wanted to do, and under any other circumstances Magdalys would have happily let her smash an escaping slave ship to smithereens. But not this time. *Slowwwwww, mama, slow. You can take it out, just don't take it all the way out.* They didn't slow, but Magdalys felt something different about Missy's roared reply. She thought maybe, maybe, she had heard her.

"Hold on, everyone!" Magdalys yelled. More gunshots

rang out as they reared up toward the *Ocarrion,* but they were too late: Missy's gigantic jaws came crashing down on the artillery unit at the far end, obliterating it and shredding a huge chunk of the hull. Magdalys, Amaya, and Redd flew up into the air but managed to stay clinging on to the saddle as Missy pulled her mouth free and slammed back into the waves beside the ship. "Good girl!" Magdalys yelled, patting Missy's neck and then following Redd and Amaya up the ladder to the deck.

On board the *Ocarrion,* chaos reigned.

A group of slavers was huddled at one end, as far from where Missy had struck as they could get, and they were firing intermittently with carbines and stabbing out with sabers when anyone got close. David Ballantine, Louis Napoleon, and a group of other Vigilance Committee agents had set up a barricade with some shipping crates at the steam chimney and were taking potshots over the top. Magdalys spotted Mapper and Two Step with them. Cymbeline stood beside them, blasting away with her shotty.

Amaya handed Magdalys a pistol and took up a position behind a crate. "Cover me," she said, snapping open her carbine and shoving a bullet into it.

Magdalys loaded up the pistol the way she'd been shown the night they escaped from the riots. She'd never had a chance to learn proper shooting with Amaya, and she certainly wasn't going to be able to learn much with everything else going on. Black powder went down the muzzle and in the chamber, then the ball went after it and you used the ramrod to pack it all in, clicked back the hammer and —

"YAAA!" came a collective roar from the far end of the *Ocarrion*. The slavers had decided to make a break for it. They poured out of their corner toward the improvised barricade. "Fire!" Louis Napoleon shouted, and gunshots rang out from either side. Several slavers collapsed where they stood or tumbled over the side, screaming. The charge made sense, Magdalys thought; they were boxed in and would either have to surrender or be massacred pretty soon.

And now they were heading straight for her. One slaver in particular, a young man with sideburns in a dark suit and a bowler hat, seemed to be staring directly at Magdalys as he charged, six-shooter raised.

She held her own pistol up, pointed at the man, held her breath, fired: *CRACK!* The blast sent tiny explosions bursting through her bones; when the smoke cleared she had no idea if she'd hit anyone or not, couldn't make out the man who'd been coming at her in the melee. Then a spray of tiny wood chips cut into Magdalys's face as a shot slammed into the crate beside her head. She looked up. The man in the bowler was closer now, raising his six-shooter again, and then an orange blur swept out of the dark sky and barreled into him, hurling him headlong into the sea with a scream and a splash.

Magdalys watched the dactyl swoop back into the night with a triumphant caw.

Ka-BANG! Amaya's rifle let out a shot. Someone screamed,

but again the smoke kept Magdalys from seeing much. She followed Amaya's example and started reloading fast. She had a dagger, and a fierce bayonet extended from the end of Amaya's rifle, but Magdalys wasn't sure what she'd do if it came to hand-to-hand combat. Throw herself over the side of the ship, probably. Death by drowning had to be better than letting some wretched slaver gut her.

BLAM! BLAM! sang Cymbeline's double-barrel shotgun. Then someone whooshed past with a *shliiiiing* of steel releasing from a scabbard and Magdalys heard yelling. Redd had jumped blade-first into the fray, his cutlass a glint of steel dancing through the night. He cleaved a path straight through the cluster of slavers, shoving and slicing as men fell screaming to either side until finally the last few survivors threw down their weapons and raised their hands, crying for mercy.

"The ship is ours!" Louis yelled.

"Hoorah!" everyone cheered.

Magdalys hugged Amaya as hard as she could. They made their way down a short flight of stairs to the main deck, where David and the Committee agents were already hog-tying their new captives. "Where are the others?" she asked.

"Sabeen is below," Cymbeline said. "We sent her to check on the kidnapped orphans. Nice work with the mosasaurus!"

Magdalys waved away the compliment. "Missy did all the work, we were just along for the ride."

Cymbeline raised an eyebrow. "Missy, huh?"

"Plus, Redd helped. Where is he anyway? He was amazing

out there." She searched the deck, caught sight of him glaring back toward the city through his spyglass.

The cabin door opened and a group of kids Magdalys recognized from the orphanage poured out, looking stunned. "Sabeen!" Amaya yelled, running across the deck and embracing her as she emerged. Magdalys dashed over too and they all hugged, and then Two Step was there and Mapper and everyone was shouting and finding their friends and making sure they were okay.

"Uh, guys," Redd called from his spot staring out at the waves. "There are lights out there. A bunch of 'em. And they're coming toward us fast."

CHAPTER THIRTY-ONE
SEA FLIGHT

EVERYONE STARTED YELLING at once. Some of the orphans, still shook up from being held captive, burst into tears.

"Man the artillery!"

"The artillery's busted!"

"Someone get the steam engine back up!"

"On it!"

"Open the sails!"

Magdalys stood beside Cymbeline and David as they glared out at the dozen lights floating toward them in pairs over the water.

"What you think?" Cymbeline said.

"I think we don't have many options. Whatever it is, I

doubt it's good and we're hobbled right now. Magdalys, start loading the kids onto the mosasaurus."

"I'm not sure how many —"

"Take as many as you can," David said. "We'll take the rest. We split up, meet back at the Red Hook shipyards, not Manhattan. That's where they'll be expecting us. Got it?"

Magdalys nodded.

"And Magdalys, I mean this: You can't take them all on. We don't even know what's out there. Just get the kids to safety, okay? As many as you can."

She nodded again, grudgingly. He was right, and she knew it. "I will."

She wanted to burst into tears and hug David and tell him it would all be alright, and then for him to say he knew it would and hug her back, but it probably wouldn't, and anyway, they didn't have time for all that.

"Load up and prepare for battle," David hollered as Magdalys hurried off to gather the orphans and start boarding.

A heavy boom percussed the sky. Mortar fire. The sea exploded a few feet away from the *Ocarrion*. "They're firing on us!" someone yelled. "Hoist the sails and prepare for evasive maneuvers!"

"Listen everyone," Magdalys said, reaching the mass of kids, "we've got to split up. I'm going to take all the youngest ones." She gazed at the wide eyes staring back at her. "Everyone younger than ten, come with me." They started separating themselves out, some still whimpering and wiping tears away.

"What if you don't know how old you are?" someone asked.

"With me," Magdalys said. "Amaya, Mapper, stay with these guys. Keep 'em safe and together. I'm taking the younger ones on Missy. We'll meet back up at the Red Hook shipyards."

Another boom sounded and then an explosion rocked the far end of the *Ocarrion* as splintered wood flew through the air. Magdalys's stomach clenched. For a moment, all she wanted to do was jump overboard and be gone. But there were other kids, other lives at stake. "Come on!" she yelled, noticing that by some miracle her voice didn't sound shaky at all. In fact, it sounded commanding. Fierce even. "My group to the mosasaurus!"

She nodded at Amaya and Mapper, trying not to think about how she might never see them again, then hurried to the edge of the ship and began helping the young ones climb down to Missy.

"Plesiosaur-mounted artillery units!" Redd yelled. He'd scaled one of the masts up to the crow's nest and was still staring out through his spyglass. "Six of 'em!"

Magdalys prayed none of those cannons hit the mast he was on top of. Ten kids had already made it onto Missy's back and they were running out of room for the sixteen that remained.

Out in the water, Magdalys could see the long dark necks between the lanterns, just like the sauropod ferries but far more lethal. Another boom shook the world and an explosion of water not far away hurled up into the air, soaking Magdalys and the others.

"Grab onto the saddle straps," she called. "And buddy up! No one's allowed to fall overboard!" Some of them chuckled, others cried. There was no space left, and ten little ones still stood anxiously on the deck of the *Ocarrion,* realization dawning on their faces.

"Greetings, my friends!" Riker's voice called out over the water.

Magdalys cringed. He must've been yelling through a bullhorn.

"I'm afraid it seems you're trapped." Riker's voice seethed with gleeful triumph.

The *Ocarrion*'s steam engine suddenly roared to life with a fitful chug-a-lug.

"If you try to resist or escape," Riker yelled, "you will be destroyed."

"You have to stay," Magdalys whispered to the ten kids. "I'm sorry. I'll do everything I can to make sure you're safe. But now I have to get these kids out of here."

"Come on," Amaya said, appearing from behind and guiding them back to the other group.

Once again, Magdalys was struck with the heart-wrenching feeling that she shouldn't be there, shouldn't be alive, shouldn't be the one to get away.

"Go!" Amaya whispered sharply as the kids hurried off. "*Now!*"

Magdalys watched her escort the last few young ones belowdecks.

"Do you have nothing to say for yourselves?" Riker taunted. "Does that mean you surrender and will give back the property you've stolen from us?"

Property, Magdalys thought. That's all people like Riker saw when they looked at them. Objects to be bought, sold, discarded, destroyed.

She barely touched the ladder going down, landed squarely on the tiny bit of space left for her at the front of Missy's saddle. She grabbed the reins.

"We have only this to say," David Ballantine yelled from the deck of the *Ocarrion* as Magdalys leaned in and jolted the reins, spurring Missy into motion.

Her eyes met David's as she sped away. Then he turned back to the approaching plesiosaurs and yelled: "Open fire!"

CHAPTER THIRTY-TWO
CHASE BACK TO THE HARBOR

EVERYTHING EXPLODED AROUND Magdalys as she sped off on mosback, sixteen squirming, whimpering orphans huddled together behind her on a saddle made for less than half that many full-sized adults.

Don't look back, Magdalys warned herself. *Don't do it. The motion is forward. Only forward.*

But she wasn't even good at following her own commands.

Flashes of musket and shotgun fire burst from the *Ocarrion* as it rattled off at a moderate pace in the opposite direction from her. Two plesiosaur artillery units had peeled off after her; she could see the glow of their lanterns shivering in the ocean breeze and hear their riders yelling back and forth. An explosion rocked the *Ocarrion,* which answered it with more small arms fire.

Magdalys put it all behind her and urged Missy forward toward the twinkling lights of New York City.

The first artillery shot went wide, way wide. Behind them, Magdalys heard one of the riders curse and realized they'd made it much closer to her than she'd thought. Which meant the next shot wouldn't be nearly so off.

She yanked the reins hard, pulling Missy off to the left just as another blast rang out, bursting through the water just inches from where they'd just been. Magdalys shook her head and spun the mosasaurus back toward their original path, then cut even further to the right. Another shot blasted out, then another, each coming within a few feet of them.

Some of the kids in the saddle behind her were shouting and crying now, while others tried to calm them down.

They couldn't keep dodging forever, Magdalys thought. Another blast blew through the water just to her right, and then one hit to her left, both closer than any of the others had been. Swimming in this zigzag pattern was slowing them down; there was no way they'd lose their pursuers like this. But if she burned a straight path to the harbor they'd be an easy shot for the artillery.

She clenched her teeth, driving hard forward for as long as she dared and then dodging to the side just in time to avoid a burst of artillery.

She had to turn and face them. That was the only way. David had expressly told her not to, and she had really meant it when she'd agreed. But this was a whole other situation; she had no choice. With a sudden jerk, Magdalys pulled them around in a full fierce circle, preparing to charge, and scanned the darkness.

The plesiosaurs were gone. Or at least their lanterns were out. Breathing heavily, Magdalys squinted into the night, saw nothing at all.

"Anybody see anything?" she asked.

The kids had stopped crying, and now she felt their collective attention turn toward the empty waters around them.

"Uh-uh," one of them said.

"Nothing."

At any second, a shell could just come hurtling out of the sky and demolish them. Magdalys calmed her breathing and waited. If she was going to face a fiery death she wanted to do so head-on, not running.

Nothing.

She waited a few beats more, and still: nothing.

"Alright," she said, turning Missy back toward the city lights. "I guess we lost 'em?"

"I dunno," one of the kids said from behind her. "Maybe they hiding."

"That's what I'm worried about. Keep sharp eyes out behind, everyone. You guys are the rear guard. See anything, and I do mean anything, you let me know. Got it?"

She realized as she spoke that she sounded just like David.

"Yes, ma'am," they all called.

"Good."

She wondered if she'd ever see him again.

The Red Hook shipyards looked more brightly lit than she'd imagined them to be, Magdalys thought as they approached. *Safety.* It was a flickering thought, but there was no doubt about it: In the tiny time she'd been there, Brooklyn had already become a kind of shelter. A small smile crossed Magdalys's face.

Then her heart plummeted.

Those weren't the regular harbor lights; they were the twin lanterns of the plesiosaur artillery units. Riker's men had peeled off so they could regroup at the harbor and form a blockade. Magdalys should've sped back the rest of the way instead of creeping in all careful. They'd probably trailed her from afar and then sped ahead when they figured out where she was going, sending messages to the others with minidacts.

And they'd seen her. She was sure of that. They'd have been watching with spyglasses, preparing, and now she could hear them calling back and forth, readying their intercept.

There were probably more of them at the Manhattan harbor, laying a secondary trap.

All that planning and Riker had still outmaneuvered them,

Magdalys thought. She rose up in the saddle, stretching her tired legs, then spurred Missy forward.

She hoped the rest of the Dactyl Hill Squad was okay, somehow.

But if she was being honest with herself, it didn't seem likely.

Forward, she urged Missy. *Full speed.*

Missy surged into motion, her tail thrashing back and forth furiously, propelling them toward the blockade with dizzying speed.

Behind her, some of the kids started wailing again.

Up ahead, the plesiosaur riders were probably readying their artillery, or simply loading their muskets to enfilade them as soon as they were in range.

Magdalys narrowed her eyes, leaning forward even further, her face just inches above Missy's slick hide. *Charge!* she silently screamed. *And destroy.*

Destroy.

They blasted into the lights of the city, the harbor torches sending their luminous shimmer across the dark waters. Missy opened her jaw in preparation for the attack. Magdalys could make out the faces of Riker's men as she raced toward them. They weren't moving, weren't preparing to fire.

Something was wrong.

Then, up on the dock, she spotted Riker himself, his long cloak and smug smile.

Something was very wrong.

Magdalys pulled back on the reins just as the plesios started to slowly float out of the way. Missy hardly noticed, just hurtled forward full speed, a magnificent roar issuing from her wide-open maw.

It was a trap, but not the kind Magdalys had thought.

This was much worse.

With the plesios out of the way, Magdalys could see clearly what had been behind them: a platform floating just in front of the Red Hook pier. Ten people stood on the platform in chains. Seven were orphans; Magdalys was pretty sure she recognized Amaya among them as she sped forward. Three were adults: Cymbeline, David, Louis.

Magdalys yanked the reins back as hard as she could, but it was no use: Missy charged forward unabated.

Missy, STOP!! Magdalys commanded, but the whole world filled with Missy's roar, her hunger for destruction, her gnashing teeth.

At the last second, Magdalys yanked the reins to the left and Missy swerved, just barely missing the platform and instead plowing into one of the columns holding up the pier, smashing it to pieces and still surging through the water like a 400-ton artillery shell.

They blew past two of the plesios, Missy clobbering one with her tail and broadsiding the other, sending it and its riders collapsing into the water. Gunshots started blasting around them, pops from the piers and matching splashes in the water. A few landed with wet, sickening thumps in Missy's hide.

None of the kids cried out, which hopefully meant they hadn't been hit, but the others had been captured. All of them. And Magdalys had almost killed them. She'd almost killed the people she loved.

Missy yelped as another musket ball slammed into her. She reared up, eager to turn and devour the pesky humans that were firing at her. Magdalys tightened her grip on the reins and pulled hard, yanking Missy back into a straight-ahead dash out into the darkness of the bay and away.

CHAPTER THIRTY-THREE
CRY HAVOC

OUT OF BREATH, exhausted, terrified, heartbroken, Magdalys rounded the corner to the street the Bochinche was on and stopped in her tracks. Behind her, the weary orphans halted as well.

"What is it?" one of the ten-year-olds, a girl named Gemma, whispered.

What indeed.

A lone raptor stood in the shadowy stable area, devouring some small pest with messy chomps and snorfs. Worse, even in the dim light of the gas lanterns, Magdalys was pretty sure she recognized that emaciated trunk and those dingy feathers. A clawless foot held down its prey. Magdalys shook her head. This was the same busted dino the head of the Rusty Raptors had been on when they'd clashed the night of the riots.

What was he doing at the Bochinche?

It barely mattered. They'd been slogging along dim backstreets for what felt like forever because Magdalys didn't want to risk being spotted by Riker's men on the commuter brachys. They were bone-tired and had nowhere else to go. Magdalys drew her pistol and motioned them to stay quiet as they approached the wooden door.

"If I say *run*, you scatter," she whispered. "Clear?"

They nodded, wide-eyed. She knocked once, then twice more, the way Cymbeline had, and waited, pistol cocked beneath her cloak.

When the door creaked open and Bernice's face appeared, Magdalys nearly broke down in tears. "Magdalys!" Bernice gasped. "Thank god, child! We were so worried!"

We?

Magdalys hugged Bernice with all her might, then stood to the side to show her she hadn't come alone. Bernice blinked. "Oh my . . . stars . . . Come in, children! Come in!"

And in they went.

The Bochinche was empty except for three figures crowded around a table: Redd, Two Step, and Mapper. Magdalys didn't know who to hug first or what to say. Two Step and Mapper solved that problem by running up and bear-hugging her before she could get a word out. Bernice led the rescued children upstairs to the bedrooms while Redd hurried over to welcome Magdalys.

"What happened?" she asked, when everyone had calmed down enough to catch their breath and settle back in around the table.

Redd shook his head. "We got got, it seems. After you and the young ones made it clear, we opened up on 'em and made a break for it. We took out two of those plesios but were getting hammered pretty bad. David put me and a bunch of the kids in the escape boat with these two hooligans and off we went, real quiet like. The Kidnapping Club was so busy bombarding the *Ocarrion* they didn't even notice."

"And the others?" Magdalys said. "I saw them at the Brooklyn docks, they were chained up . . ." The terrifying thought of how close she'd come to killing the people she loved reared back up in her mind. She shoved it away.

"Captured," Two Step said. "And now Riker has 'em at the Penitentiary."

"The one right there on top of Dactyl Hill?" Magdalys gaped. "Wha — how?"

"We followed 'em," Mapper said. "Once we got away we made for the docks, snuck up and watched from the shadows while they transported them on a brachy."

"Along the way we bumped into an ol' friend of mine," Redd put in. "And by friend I mean 'guy I once robbed.' Seems he got run out of the Raptor Claw after word got around he'd been bested by a black girl with a shotgun during the riots . . ."

"The Rusty Raptor guy!" Magdalys almost spat.

"Yeah, him. He was still butthurt about the whole thing, ranting and raving in the streets. So I robbed him again."

"*That's* why his raptor's outside."

Redd shook his head earnestly. "Poor thing was near starving and ol' boy was spending his money on drink. I really did everyone a favor, to be honest."

"Especially us," Mapper said. "Without that raptor we never would've been able to keep up with the transport brachy."

"Anyway," Redd said, "we figure Riker's holding 'em at the Dactyl Hill Pen because the *Ocarrion*'s wrecked and he has no other way to transport 'em out the city for now," Redd said. "Probably will by the end of tomorrow though."

Magdalys felt her heart start to zoom. "We have to —"

"Break 'em out?" Mapper said. "Already on it." He pulled out a big sheet of parchment that he must've shoved under the table when they heard someone at the door.

Magdalys's eyes went wide. "The Penitentiary!"

Mapper had rendered it in explicit detail, as only he could. Little numbers estimated the lengths of each wall (not that those numbers would be much help to anyone *but* Mapper, Magdalys thought). He'd even approximated the artillery reach from each of the gun turrets on the towers and signified with dotted lines how he guessed the different inner chambers would be laid out.

"I still don't understand how little dude did this," Redd said.

"He flew over it when we were dactyling from rooftop to rooftop sweeping chimneys," Magdalys explained.

"Yeah, but . . ." Redd gestured at the intricacy of Mapper's sketch.

Two Step shrugged. "He's Mapper. But ay, how we gonna bust up into that place, get past the guards, through that gigantic door, find our friends, and get 'em out?"

Everyone looked back and forth for a moment, and then the door from the back room flew open and Halsey Crunk stormed in, with Josephine in tow. Both were armed to the teeth. "The fire-eyed maid of smoky war," Halsey declared, "all hot and bleeding will we offer them!"

Miss Josephine rolled her eyes. "'E 'as been talking like this ever since you all came back and told 'im Mademoiselle Cymbeline had been captured. Ah! Magdalys, mon cherie, I am so glad to see you are alright!" She blew Magdalys a kiss and then set about loading the Winchester she was carrying.

"Whoa," Mapper said. "You guys raided the secret artillery closet?"

A whole arsenal of weaponry was dangling or strapped to the two of them. "The arms are fair," Halsey said, cleaning off a Winchester, "when the intent of bearing them is just."

"Totally didn't answer my question," Mapper muttered.

"Madame Bernice let us in," Josephine explained. "As to where she got them, she did not wish to elaborate and I did not press 'er for information."

"Alright," Redd said, "we can figure this out on the way,

but let's get moving. I want the Penitentiary staked out so we can see what's what from there."

They all stood. The night seemed suddenly ready to burst with all that was about to happen. Magdalys felt her pulse thrumming through her ears as she wove her braids into a bun behind her head and took a deep breath.

"Cry 'havoc,'" Halsey whispered, "and let slip the dactyls of war."

Magdalys rolled her eyes and then everyone bustled out the door.

CHAPTER THIRTY-FOUR
STAKEOUT

THEY LOADED THE weapons stash onto the raptor (who Redd informed them was named Reba) and made their way quietly through the midnight streets of Dactyl Hill, glancing around for slinking shadows or dinoriders at each turn.

The flaming wall torches of the Penitentiary seemed to glare angrily as they approached, until finally Redd motioned for everyone to huddle out of sight at the side of an old stucco-walled factory. He peered out. "Okay, so we're up against an armored fortress, with how many knucklehead-riding guards did you say, Mapper?"

Mapper pulled out the floor plans he'd drawn and unrolled them. "Two at each gun turret, four at the front gate, two walking the walls, so at least eight on a normal night."

"And they have shotguns," Magdalys added, remembering the way those double-barrels had glistened in the sun as the knuckleskulls strutted clunkily along the fortress rampart.

"Fantastic," Redd said. "I see three guys at the front right now, none on dinos. But these are Kidnapping Clubbers, not regular prison guards. They got cloaks and rifles. That means we can probably count on more of 'em being inside."

"For sure," Mapper said, narrowing his eyes at the drawing as if a master attack plan would materialize if he just squinted it into existence.

Magdalys looked over the motley crew that had gathered. "And against that, we got . . ."

"A pirate," Redd said. "A map wizard. A dinowrangler. An actor."

Halsey bowed extra low to the ground. "Do not discount the actor, good sir, for murder, though it have no tongue, will speak with most miraculous organ!"

Redd pursed his lips. "Okay, but do it quietly, please. We still relying on the element of surprise and all that."

"Right." Halsey lowered his voice to a stage whisper. "Also, I'm a crack shot with a Springfield . . ."

"Cool."

"Now that I am sober."

"Alright, man. And . . . you in, Miss Josephine?"

"But of course, mon cherie! I am here, am I not?"

"And a Haitian pyrotechnic specialist."

She grinned wickedly. "Ooh, I like this!"

"And a kid named Two Step."

Two Step made finger guns. "That's the title of my autobiography, actually."

"Plus a bunch of weapons," Magdalys said.

"And let's not forget Reba," Redd said.

"Plus whatever dactyls we can rustle up," Mapper added.

Magdalys shook her head. It wasn't enough. It was never enough. After all their planning and caution with the *Ocarrion* raid, it had still blown up in their faces. How were they supposed to take on a whole fortress with no time to plan and barely any kind of team at all? "Riker had at least a dozen men tonight, and who knows how many more? We're outnumbered for sure."

Redd chuckled sadly. "Yeaaah, the pirate's life, hey. Outgunned and outmanned, cuz. We gotta be slippery. Once we in, Halsey and Miss Josephine head to one side and I'll hit the other. The cells line the courtyard facing inward and they got little windows on the doors. I may not be Mapper but I remember that much from my little stint in there. Gotta snatch the keys from one of these door guards and then bust out our folks when we find 'em. The real question is, how do we get inside?"

"Let's march without the noise of threatening drum," Halsey said.

Redd nodded. "Right. A sneak attack."

"Then sound trumpets! Let our bloody colors wave!"

"I really need you to keep it down, man."

"And either victory, or else a gra —"

"Enough," Miss Josephine declared, shoving Halsey out of the way. "We send in Monsieur Crunk to distract them, oui? Then myself and Monsieur Redd 'roll up' as you say on Rebus —"

"Reba."

"— from opposite ends of the street and overwhelm them and open the gates. Meanwhile, les enfants land on one of the parapets avec les dactyls, take control of the artillery, and provide backup fire when we enter the yard."

"Enfants is children," Two Step whispered to Magdalys.

She rolled her eyes. "I know that, man!"

"Then we bust everyone free and fight our way out as needed," Redd said. "It's tight, but it might work. It just might work."

Magdalys couldn't see it, but her whole body screamed to do something, anything, to get her friends free. "Alright," she said. "It's bonkers, but we don't have much choice. Give us ten minutes to get into position and grab some dactyls. Mapper, go with Miss Josephine and then head up. Redd, Two Step and I will roll with you and then hit the roofs."

CHAPTER THIRTY-FIVE
PARAPET SWOOP

"SO WHAT IS it, Magdalys?" Redd said as they slipped around a corner through the shadows.

"What's what?"

"That something special you got with the dinos."

Magdalys felt her heart rate speed up a fraction. She wasn't sure why — there was plenty of danger around and all of it worse than admitting what she'd never said out loud before: that she could hear the dinos' thoughts and control them with her mind. "I guess I'm just a good wrangler," Magdalys muttered. "I don't know, really."

"This one's open," Two Step whispered from a doorway up ahead.

"I'm right behind you," Magdalys said. Two Step nodded and disappeared inside.

"Hold up, cuz," Redd said, his hand landing on Magdalys's shoulder.

She glanced around. Had he seen something? "What is it?"

"That ain't how power works."

"What?"

"You can't mumble bout it. What you scared of?"

Magdalys shook her head. "I don't understand."

"Shame, girl. I'm talking bout shame. What's your magic? Why you scared of it?"

"I'm . . . I'm not. We gotta go though."

"We got a sec before the attack. I've never seen anyone wrangle a mosasaur like you did. Most folks can't even get near 'em without losing a limb, let alone ride it like they were born to. What's your magic?"

"It's not . . . it's not magic. It's just that I can . . . I can hear the dinos. Like, in my head? And, when I think . . . they do what I tell them. Mostly." Magdalys was staring at the cobblestones, which still glistened from the rain showers earlier.

Redd let out a wild cackle. Magdalys looked up, frown already stretched across her face. She'd finally admitted the secret she'd never told anyone and Redd was laughing at her?

"That's amazing!" Redd said. "You're like . . . a dinogenius!"

Magdalys raised her eyebrows. "I mean . . ."

"Like those old-time back-in-the-day dinowarriors everyone talk about. Girl, say it loud. Otherwise how you gonna get even better at it?"

It hadn't even occurred to Magdalys that she could get

better at it. When she met Redd's eyes they'd turned serious, the laughter suddenly gone.

"I wasn't born in a body most people would call a boy's," Redd said. "I had to, you know, learn not to let what other folks thought of me determine how I thought about myself."

Magdalys nodded. She couldn't understand what that must've been like, but she knew how powerful names were.

"I had to learn to say, *Ay — my name is Redd and I don't care what you think! Every bit of me a boy!* I mean, didn't stop certain people from wanting to kill me for who I was, so I still had to get good with a cutlass, but it helped me figure out what matters and what don't."

"Mags, you coming?" Two Step called from the doorway.

"Coming," Magdalys said, still looking Redd in his big brown eyes.

Redd grinned. "Feel me?"

Magdalys did, she definitely did. "Hey, Two Step," she said, a smile creeping across her face.

"Huh?"

"My name's Magdalys Roca."

"I know, Mags, what's going o —"

"And I can wrangle dinos with my mind."

"Oh snap! I mean, I kinda figured. But cool! Can we, uh, can we go storm the prison now?"

Magdalys and Two Step had just reached the edge of a nearby rooftop when they heard Halsey's voice from down below on the street.

"Give me the cups," he called. "And let the kettle to the trumpet speak!"

"Halt, you!" a gruff voice called out.

"The cannons to the heavens, the heavens to earth."

"Halt, I say."

"Now the king dunkth to Hamlet."

"Oh, man, he's wasted," another guard groaned. "Get him out of here."

"Or just throw him inside and be done with it," a third said. The others laughed. "Stay sharp, lads. The Magistrate said to be on the lookout for any funny stuff."

So Riker was there, Magdalys thought. Or had been.

Redd's laughter-tinged voice rose up in the night: "Funny like this?" Magdalys peered over, caught sight of him and Josephine riding Reba straight toward the Penitentiary gate, guns blazing. Halsey flung himself out of the way as shotgun blasts and pistol shots filled the night.

"Get back!" one of the guards called.

"I'm hit!"

"Don't let up, men!"

Magdalys heard a terrible roar from somewhere nearby. *What on earth was that?* Didn't matter: The gunshots were their cue. "Go," she whispered. "Go!" Two Step and Magdalys ran side by side across the rooftop toward the dark cluster of shapes at the other end. "That middle one," Magdalys said. "The tallest."

"Got it," Two Step said.

"One," she counted as they sprinted closer and closer to the dactyl squad. "Two . . . and jump!" Magdalys went for the neck and Two Step hurled onto the dactyl's torso. It squawked, bursting forward, and flapped out into the sky. Below them, more shots rang out, and Magdalys prayed Redd, Halsey, and Josephine were okay.

Off to their left, a shadowy shape soared past and then dipped sharply down. Mapper.

Circle the tower, Magdalys commanded, and their dactyl cut a wide arc and then spiraled toward the parapet. Below them, flickering torches lit the open Penitentiary yard. There were shapes in there, large ones. Dinos. It spun past too fast for her to figure out what, but they looked wide and squat and — *BLAM!!* Two Step's carbine burst to life behind her. The shot pinged off the wall, but it was enough to get the attention of the guard manning the howitzer. *BLAM!!* The carbine fired again, this time dinging the artillery unit itself.

Magdalys brought them in low for his next shot, which smashed into the wall just close enough to the gunner for him to get the picture. He threw himself on the ground and crawled away. "Nice shooting," Magdalys said, swinging the dactyl for one more circle over the walls.

"Trikes!" Two Step yelled, and Magdalys knew without another glance that's what those shapes had been. The

Kidnapping Club had brought in a battalion of tricera-topses, a beast reserved almost exclusively for use by the War Department, at least when they were young and healthy.

She landed on the parapet. The mighty dinos stood in military formation, each with additional armor supplementing its already fierce horned head shield and thick hide. More goons from the Kidnapping Club sat astride each trike, rifled muskets trained on the front gate.

The front gate that Redd, Halsey, and Miss Josephine were about to bust through. It was going to be a massacre.

On the far wall, Mapper landed his own dactyl and gazed down in disbelief. Then he locked eyes with Magdalys. She could see he knew what they both had to do. There wasn't time to work the howitzers; the door would swing open at any moment. "Get ready to shoot, Two Step," Magdalys said. She nodded slightly at Mapper, then they both launched their dac-tyls into a nosedive at the waiting trike battalion below.

CHAPTER THIRTY-SIX

ATTACK!

MAGDALYS LET OUT a fierce cry as the night wind whipped through her hair. The trike riders looked up, some of their hoods falling back to reveal startled, angry faces. It wasn't enough for them to look, though; she needed those guns trained away from the gate.

From nearby, Mapper let out his own battle cry, and then Two Step's carbine started blasting away right behind her. And then they were zipping just a few feet over the dusty ground, Magdalys leaning low so Two Step could get a clear shot over her head, and the trike riders were raising their rifles but it was too late, she'd already zoomed into their ranks, between the rows of those great red-and-gray beasts, shouts and gunshots erupting around her, her whole body a tight fist, bracing, bracing for the vicious shock of a bullet ripping through her.

And then they were back up in the sky, more shots ringing out from below, the sharp whistle of a ball slinging past them into the night, the thrill of having made it mixed with the terror of knowing it wasn't over, it was never over.

When they'd glided out of range, she looped back around and there, down below, was the first tiny victory of the attack: The gates had swung wide open and, even better, Halsey, Josephine, and Redd were nowhere to be seen. That meant they'd probably slipped in during the confusion and were setting to work freeing the entire Penitentiary.

Meanwhile, chaos already reigned in the yard, as two of the trikes thundered toward each other, spooked and furious, and a third stumbled to one side, nearly throwing its rider. "Now let's see about that howitzer," Magdalys said. There was a sonorous boom from below and something huge whizzed past just a few inches away.

"I think someone already did," Two Step said.

Another boom sounded and Magdalys swerved the dactyl into a sharp turn and then swooped low. How many times would she have to dodge mortar fire in one night? From the corner of her eye, she caught sight of Mapper making another swing through the yard as rifles crackled to life around him. And then his dactyl let out a shriek and crumpled, tumbling through a sudden explosion of dirt.

"No!" Magdalys yelled, already swerving them into a steep dive toward where Mapper lay beneath his downed mount.

"Is he alive?" Two Step said over the whistling wind and

popping rifles. She didn't know and didn't have it in her to answer anyway. "Cover me," was all she could get out through her clenched jaw. Two Step let off three blasts as they skidded to a halt beside Mapper. The dactyl lay dead; a rifle shot had taken half its head off. Magdalys gasped. Mapper stirred beneath it, unconscious but alive.

"Let's get him," Magdalys yelled, dismounting. Two Step was right behind her, and then more shots slammed into the dirt in front of them and the ground shook. When Magdalys looked up, an armored triceratops was thundering toward her, its sharp beak-like snout inches above the ground, those three horns aimed directly at Magdalys. Yells sounded from somewhere nearby, but everything seemed to move in slow motion. The trike bore down on them; the cloaked rider raised his rifle, and then a shot rang out from right next to Magdalys. She flinched. Up ahead, the rider had slumped forward and now his limp body was sliding from the saddle. Magdalys looked up from her crouch. Two Step hadn't lowered his carbine; he just stood there, eyes wide, mouth slightly open. The trike had barely slowed its roll, and now was bearing down on them with renewed vigor as more shooting erupted at the far side of the yard.

Then a purple-brown blur blitzed in from the side, landing on the charging beast.

"Reba!" Magdalys yelled. "Redd!" The slender raptor skittered across the trike's rump with surprising agility, sending both reeling into a sharp turn.

"Heeyah!" Redd yelled, taking a few potshots from the top of his now dinoriding dino. The trike spun a wild circle beneath them, dust billowing in all directions.

Two Step still hadn't lowered the gun. For a second she was worried he'd been hit by some flying debris or something, but then he spoke and she understood. "I killed him," Two Step muttered. "That man."

The trike rider was indeed lying crumpled in the dirt about ten feet from them.

"Two Step," Magdalys said, "he was going to kill you. He was going to kill me. You saved my life."

He seemed to snap out of it a little, finally lowering the rifle, but his eyes still stared at some nonexistent point in the distance.

"And now we gotta get Mapper out of here, man." *And you too,* she thought, casting a worried glance at her friend's wide-open face. "Come on." He stumbled over to the dactyl corpse with Magdalys. Seeing Mapper unconscious beneath it brought Two Step back around even more. Together, they heaved the dust and blood-covered ptero off to the side and then hoisted Mapper up and brought him to where their dactyl waited anxiously.

"Get him on," Magdalys ordered. "Hurry." A shotgun blast exploded nearby and Magdalys jumped out of the way. On the parapet above, the knuckleskull-mounted prison guards were filing in at a lopsided canter. They seemed to be shooting at random into the courtyard below.

"Mags!" Redd yelled from a few feet away. "Heads up!" She looked, bracing to meet some new attack head-on. Instead, a huge set of keys flew through the air toward her. The door guard keys. Redd's toss went high, but she swatted them into the dust and then scooped them up. "We can't hold off these trikes for long," Redd said. Behind him, Halsey Crunk and Miss Josephine were ducking behind a pillar, poking out every few seconds to pick off their attackers. Halsey wasn't kidding when he said he was a crack shot — every time his Springfield rang out, a cry and thud sounded from across the yard. "Take the keys and get our folks! Now! We'll cover you!"

Magdalys barely had time to nod before Redd spun Reba around one more time on top of the trike and then sent her leaping off, directly into the fray as shotgun blasts erupted around them.

When she turned back, Two Step was backed all the way against the wall, eyes wide, head shaking back and forth. Mapper lay slumped across the dactyl. Magdalys pocketed the keys and ran over to Two Step. "You gotta go, man. You gotta . . . Listen to me! Get Mapper out of here. Go back to the Bochinche and tell Miss Bernice to call for a doctor." Her voice sharpened and he finally blinked and turned to her. "Two Step?"

He nodded, face stricken. "I . . . I can't leave you guys."

"You have to, man. You can't help us right now. Mapper needs you." He shook his head, then nodded. She guided him to the ptero, which was nuzzling its fallen squadmate and stomping its feet. "I know, big fella," Magdalys said, patting its snout as she helped Two Step climb on. "I'm so sorry." *Take my friends back to the Bochinche,* she thought. *And then don't let them come back here no matter what.*

A series of blasts rang out, but Magdalys couldn't make out what was happening through the smoke and dust. "Go!" she yelled. "Go!"

CHAPTER THIRTY-SEVEN
ABRE CAMINO

MAGDALYS MADE A breathless dash to the nearest wall, sliding into the dust beneath the walkway and then skittering behind a pillar as an artillery shell blew out a chunk of wall a few feet away. Tiny shards of rock and mortar splattered her face. "What's going on out there?" someone screamed. Magdalys could make out a group of figures through the bars on the door directly in front of her.

She stood, dusting herself off. "Is Cymbeline in there?" It didn't look like any kids were there. But maybe . . . "Or someone named David Ballantine?"

"Cymba who now?"

"Man, we don't know no David."

"But get us out of here!"

"Yeah!"

Magdalys gazed down the long wall of barred cell doors. There were at least a dozen on this side alone. Out in the courtyard, a group of knuckleskulls had come down from the upper walkway and were swarming toward where Miss Josephine and Halsey had holed up. Redd was nowhere to be seen. She looked back at the cell in front of her.

"Girl?" someone said. "Will you help us?"

Magdalys dug out the keys. "If you help me." Cheers erupted as she shoved one key and then another into the lock. "When I open this," she said, "I need you to take these keys and open all the other ones. Got it?"

"Ha! We with it!"

"Who is this girl? Someone give her a medal!"

Magdalys grimaced. "You're not free yet." But even as she said it, the key she was holding slid into place with a click and the barred door swung open. Magdalys pulled the keys out and stepped out of the way as a flood of prisoners surged out. A tall, wide man with one eye and trembling hands towered over her. "I'm Tiny Shanks," he said, breaking into a grin. "Pass me those keys and I'll handle the rest of those prison cells for you. And thanks!"

Magdalys held out the keys to him. She wondered what crime, if any, this man had committed to be locked up here. Cops seemed to arrest black folks at random most of the time, just scooping people up and carting them off for the most nonsensical offenses.

Tiny Shanks took the keys with a doff of his imaginary cap

and then ran off. Magdalys threw herself against the wall, panting. Pretty soon, newly freed inmates flooded the yard.

"Mags!" a familiar voice yelled. Magdalys looked up to see Sabeen and Amaya running toward her. Cymbeline was right behind them, a nasty bruise on her forehead but otherwise okay.

"Are you guys okay?" Magdalys gasped as they all embraced quickly and then hurried out of the way of a rush of inmates swarming a knuckleskull rider.

Cymbeline shook her head. "We are now. Where's Halsey?"

"Over —" Magdalys started to say, but a monstrous growl erupted from the front gate, cutting her off. A gigantic shadow lurked beyond it, just out of sight. Magdalys gasped.

A tyrannosaurus stomped into the yard, ducking forward so it could fit under the gate and then rearing up to its full height and stomping up mountain clouds of dust on either side. One man rode on its saddled back: Magistrate Richard Riker. He carried a whip and wore those long robes. A wide smile crossed his face as he urged the tyrannosaurus into the fray.

"Back!" Riker called. "You are all my prisoners! My property! Seal the entrance, men!" Two triceratops riders headed toward the gate but the mounts pulled away, spooked by the humongous carnivore. In the yard, newly freed prisoners screamed and scattered, but there was nowhere to run.

Dust blew across the yard as Riker's tyrannosaurus stomped back and forth in front of the gate, terrorizing prisoners, guards, and trike riders alike and chomping down anyone who wasn't fast enough to get out of its way.

Rifle blasts rang out, but no one could get a clear shot through the chaos.

Magdalys scrambled with Amaya and Sabeen to a far corner of the yard behind some trembling trikes as the huge dino let out another roar. Cymbeline was gone, already disappeared into the mob. They would all be torn to shreds, everyone she loved. And her.

Girl, say it loud, Redd had said. *Otherwise how you gonna get even better at it?*

So much had already happened since that moment, Magdalys had barely had time to catch her breath, let alone try and understand what he'd meant. Redd had basically told her she was the best dinowrangler he'd ever seen, so how could she get . . . better . . . ? The idea formed even as the question was still unraveling in her mind. Maybe those ancient dinoriding warriors really did exist. And maybe they did even cooler stuff with their steeds than anyone could imagine nowadays. She looked up at the three riderless trikes cowering around them. They formed a nice little barricade against the desperate fighting in the yard. But they'd make an even better battering ram. She took a step toward them, hand stretched out. The dinos were too freaked out about the tyrannosaurus to care what Magdalys was doing.

“Mags,” Amaya hissed. “What are you — ?”

“I’m Magdalys Roca,” she said. “And I’m the greatest dinowrangler the world has ever known.”

She heard Sabeen whisper, “Well, shoot,” and then Magdalys leapt up into the closest trike’s saddle. The beast startled some at first, raising its massive forelegs up and then slamming them down again. “Shhh, big guy,” Magdalys whispered. “I know you’re scared.” He calmed, and then, staying low to keep out of the way of any passing bullets or buckshot, she reached out with her mind to the other two.

At first, nothing happened, and Magdalys wondered if she was ridiculous for even considering connecting with three dinos at once. Then their whinnied replies came back in trembling vibratos. They felt her, understood what she wanted. They didn’t like it, but they knew what they had to do. With some shuffling and grumbled snorts, all three triceratopses wheeled themselves around to face the yard. Terrified though they were, these beasts had been trained. They were armored and battle-ready. Magdalys could feel that grim determination sharpen their focus as their shakiness fell away.

Out in the dust-clouded yard, Riker’s tyrannosaurus leaned down and gobbled up a man in a prison uniform, then swept its tail in a wide arc, clobbering two knuckleskulls and sending their riders flying.

All together, now, she thought. *As one.* And then, *CHARGE!!*

CHAPTER THIRTY-EIGHT
THE SHAKE 'N' DROP

PRISONERS, ORPHANS, KIDNAPPING Clubbers, and guards all scattered out of the way as Magdalys's three armored trikes thundered across the yard. Her heart galumphed along with their roaring stomps, and their combined grit and determination pulsed through her. Up ahead, Riker looked up from his rampage, his face red and scrunched with fury. He let out a yell and then urged his mount forward to meet their charge.

As the trikes closed in, the tyrannosaurus launched into the air, landing with his huge hind legs on the triceratops directly to Magdalys's left. Hers and the one to her right skidded off to the side as the poor beast collapsed with a squeal. Dust flew up around it. Riker howled with triumph. The tyrannosaurus, just a few feet away, leaned in and tore out its fallen prey's neck.

No! Magdalys thought, circling her mount back around. If she could catch it while it was still chomping, maybe . . . They rushed forward, the other trike pulling ahead and lowering its great armored head as it charged. Riker's tyrannosaurus looked up and bellowed just in time to catch a horn through its thigh. Its roar turned into a shriek of pain. Magdalys's trike hit next, its top right horn tearing a nasty gash across the larger dino's flank as they passed.

The wounded beast's roar was almost deafening. It wrenched itself free of the other trike's horn and spun, bashing the triceratops with its thick tail. Both dinos stumbled away from each other, stunned and bleeding.

"Riker!" Magdalys yelled.

"Ah, one of the little orphans," Riker sneered. He was winded and his cheeks were flushed, but that triumphant smile still spread across his face. He raised one arm, the long black sleeve of his robe dangling beneath it, and wagged a finger at Magdalys. "When will you children ever learn your place, hm?"

Magdalys just stared at him, her mount strutting a slow circle around the yard, head bowed, ready to charge.

"Well, you've already lost, my dear. We chased you out of Manhattan that night, and then we chased you out of the harbor when you tried to steal back your friends, my rightful property, and now we're chasing you out of Dactyl Hill, where you thought you were safe."

Magdalys tried to tune him out. He wanted to distract her, keep her off her game. Beneath her the trike grunted and growled in heaving snorts. He was a good, determined mount. Even after the carnage they'd just been part of, he was ready for more.

"Do you see what I'm saying, dear?" Riker taunted. "You're not safe. Not even here, up north, in the beating heart of Lincoln's anti-slavery crusade. You're not safe and you never will be. You may have burned down my associate Mr. Weed's home, you vile savage, but he's already set up operations in a new one. Our network stretches across the globe, don't you see? We are everywhere."

The Knights of the Golden Circle. What a pitiful and horrendous idea to build a secret society around. It was like Riker's Kidnapping Club times a thousand and spread across the Americas. And who would stop them? The U.S. Army was all tangled up trying to hold off the Confederates down south. And anyway, it wasn't so long ago that slavery was common practice throughout all the United States.

Magdalys kept circling as the battle raged on around them. She held her focus on Riker, but from what she could gather, things weren't going well. The prison guards and Kidnapping Clubbers had gotten it together enough to realize they were on the same team, and a bunch of the freed prisoners were simply cowering in the shadows, hoping the whole thing would just be over soon.

Riker's tyrannosaurus roared and leaned forward, chomping its huge jaws and sending Magdalys and her trike stumbling a few steps back. "Even if you get your friends free tonight," Riker yelled, "you'll know, won't you, that around every corner we wait, ready to pounce. You'll always have to watch your back, because I'll always be there, and if not me, someone else, and someone else, and someone . . ."

Magdalys had heard enough; she leaned forward, spurring her mount into a charge.

"Oh ho!" Riker chortled, pulling back on his reins. The tyrannosaurus growled, then opened its huge mouth and let out a roar. Those teeth were almost as big as Magdalys. Instead of hitting the beast head-on, she lifted to a standing crouch on the saddle and pulled the trike to the side at the last second, hurling herself onto the tyrannosaurus's back.

Around them, shots rang out as Cymbeline and Redd led the freed inmates in a desperate charge against the guards; the two sides clashed amidst growling, snorting dinos and battle cries. The tyrannosaurus spun, snapping at Magdalys as she scurried up toward Riker. The battle-strewn yard whirled around them dizzyingly as more screams and roars sounded.

Calm, Magdalys thought, trying to latch on to the mighty dino's mind. The reply was only a desperate howl within her. But it sounded more fearful than fierce. That was odd. Magdalys looked up, saw Riker grinning down at her, pulling a pistol from his belt. But behind him, something gigantic took over the sky. The tyrannosaurus had seen it, was already yelping and crouching out of the way.

Magdalys blinked, her mouth falling open. Riker turned to curse at his mount and then shrieked.

Stella the pteranodon swooped out of the night, landing with one huge claw on the neck of the tyrannosaurus, pinning it to the dusty ground. Magdalys watched the claw tighten as the dino's eyes went wide. Riker raised his pistol to the pteranodon's huge face.

"No!" Magdalys yelled, launching forward and jumping on him from behind. The gun went off, its ball blasting uselessly into the sky. Magdalys smashed Riker's gun hand against the fallen tyrannosaurus's hide as hard as she could. The pistol clattered into the dust.

"Unhand me!" Riker yelled, wrestling his wrist out of Magdalys's grip. He reached back and swung at her, but the magistrate was slow, and Magdalys dodged out of the way, feeling the side of his fist grazing her cheek as she nearly toppled from the saddle.

Instead, she gripped one of the dangling reins and used it to swing back around, smashing shoulder-first into Riker, who toppled backward. Magdalys scrambled up toward Stella, grabbing the ptero's neck just as the ground fell away beneath them, and with a tremendous flap of those forty-foot wings they lifted off.

A hand wrapped around Magdalys's foot and she screamed, glancing down.

The tyrannosaurus was still dangling from Stella's claws

and Riker still clung to its saddle with one hand, Magdalys's ankle clutched in the other. "You stupid girl," Riker yelled into the wind. "You'll never ever be safe! Don't you see?"

Up, up, up into the night they hurtled, into the sky until the Dactyl Hill Penitentiary was just a small, torchlit pit amidst the teeming city. Magdalys looked down, a strange calm settling within her. Riker seemed suddenly pathetic, clinging with all his might to her ankle. She shook her head, locking eyes with him.

"Ah, I remember you now," Riker yelled. "The little dino-wrangler! Of course. Margaret, was it? Rocheford?"

She wrenched her ankle from his grasp. "My name is Magdalys Roca."

"Stupid —"

"Handle him, Stella," Magdalys said, still staring at him. Riker's eyes went wide.

". . . girl?"

Stella gave the tyrannosaurus one mighty shake and let go, reaching down to snap Riker up in her beak as the dino fell away with a yelp.

Riker let out a gasp and then he was gone, and Stella gulped once and then swooped a circle through the clouds before diving back down. The wind whipped through Magdalys's hair, sang songs of sorrow and freedom against her face, whispered of all that had just happened and all that was yet to come, and then they were back and a mighty shout went up from the yard. Then another. "Hoorah!" everyone thundered.

Magdalys scanned the crowd beneath her. There was David Ballantine, his fist in the air, triumphant. Louis Napoleon stood beside him, grinning and shouting. Both were covered in dust and blood but seemed to be okay. The prison guards and Kidnapping Clubbers had seen what happened to their leader and fled. Sabeen and Amaya were in a far corner of the yard with a group of orphans. Amaya had pistols in each hand, both raised above her heads as she shouted with joy. Sabeen jumped up and down, screaming and hugging Miss Josephine, who just shook her head in disbelief. Cymbeline, now on trikeback with Halsey, shook her head in wonder and looked up at Magdalys. Redd and Reba hopped around giving random folks high fives and yelling at the sky.

"Let's get everyone out of here," David called out. "Before the actual cops come and start asking questions." Newly freed inmates streamed out the front gate.

Magdalys patted the pteranodon lovingly as they circled in for a gentle and still thunderous landing. "Well played, Stella girl."

Arrrooommmph, the ptero sang.

Magdalys pushed gently on Stella's neck, leaning her forward into a crouch so the approaching orphans could climb on. Then she waved at David and launched into the night.

CHAPTER THIRTY-NINE

A JOURNEY BEGINS

IT WAS ALMOST dawn. The sky had brightened ever so slightly in the east, but Brooklyn itself was still a dim, gaslight-speckled shadow world.

Magdalys stood on the rooftop. Behind her, Stella stood perched, clearly doing her best not to destroy any buildings with those monstrous claws.

Louis Napoleon and David Ballantine put four sacks down in front of Magdalys that they'd carried up on Bernice's orders. "Supplies," Bernice said, wrapping her arms around Magdalys. "There's a couple weeks' worth of hardtack in there, that's what the boys eat down south on the front, plus pterofeed in case you can't find any wandering . . . whatever that thing eats."

"Entire cities probably," David said. Stella chirped happily.

"And I know you know, but . . . please be careful." Magdalys smiled into Bernice's shoulder, thanked her.

"I know I can't persuade you to stay," David said, stepping forward.

Magdalys nodded.

"And anyway, you're probably right. They're gonna be looking for Stella here and whoever broke her free. And I know you have to find your brother." David looked out across the rooftops. "I had a brother once," he said very quietly. "Younger than me."

Magdalys hugged him tight.

"You're doing the right thing," David whispered. "And you have a good, good heart, Magdalys Roca. Don't forget that."

She squeezed him again, said, "Thank you for everything and please try to stay safe," then let him go. Louis Napoleon was next, shaking her hand and nodding like a proud dad; then Redd and Miss Josephine, who looked like she was reconsidering going back to Haiti after all the fun she'd had in Brooklyn.

Then Sabeen, Amaya, Two Step (still shook, but definitely better than earlier), and Mapper (his head bandaged, but otherwise apparently okay) walked onto the roof. They all looked dead serious, contrite even.

Magdalys swallowed hard and raised her eyebrows. The Dactyl Hill Squad had become the closest thing she'd ever known to a family besides her actual siblings. She wasn't sure how she was going to manage without them, but she knew she'd figure it out somehow. And anyway, she had to act like she was cool about it, otherwise things would just get soppy. "What's wrong, guys?"

"Nothin'," Mapper said.

"We're just sad to see you go," Sabeen added.

Two Step shook his head. "I don't even have a dance for it."

"It's just . . ." Amaya started. Then she stopped, put her hands over her face. Magdalys didn't know what to do.

"It's just," Amaya said again, her shoulders heaving up and down.

"It's just . . . I CAN'T DO THIS, YOU GUYS!" She burst out laughing.

Wait, Magdalys thought. *She's laughing?*

Two Step and Mapper both groaned and rolled their eyes.

"Are you kidding me?" Sabeen growled, stomping her foot. "Even I could pull that one off and I *suck* at jokes."

Jokes? Magdalys tilted her head at her friends. Then she spotted the rucksacks they'd all been keeping hidden behind them. "You're not . . . you guys aren't . . ."

"Of course we are," Mapper said, still shaking his head at Amaya. "And we would've been able to draw that out a lot longer if Happy McSnorfles over there hadn't ruined the whole thing by laughing." He grabbed his sack, marched past Magdalys, and loaded his supplies onto the makeshift saddle they'd put together for Stella.

"I . . . I can't believe it," Magdalys gasped.

"We a squad," Two Step said, and she'd never been so happy to see him smile. "It's how we survive."

"If you heading south to find Montez," Mapper called from the saddle, "then *we* heading south to find Montez."

"I don't know what to say," Magdalys said.

"And anyway," Mapper added, "how else you gonna know which way to fly?"

Magdalys laughed as Two Step hugged her and then two-stepped past to the ptero.

Amaya and Sabeen paused in front of Magdalys. "You saved us," Sabeen said. "Saved us all."

Magdalys shook her head. "We all saved each other more times than I can count. And anyway, Stella did all the hard work."

"Sabeen is right," Amaya said. "And you know how I feel about dinoriding, so the fact that I'm about to get on this thing for an extended sojourn means I really love you, Magdalys."

"I mean, technically it's a ptero not a dino," Magdalys said with a wink. "Buuuut I take your point." Amaya rolled her eyes and hugged her tight.

"Um, hello? Girls?"

Magdalys and Amaya looked up. Marietta Gilbert Smack stepped out from behind everyone else. "Whoa, Miss Smack!" Magdalys said. "I didn't expect you!"

"I've been helping out the Vigilance Committee," Marietta said with a wink. "And recruiting some other white women out of the Ladies' Manumission Society over to this end of the work. Good luck, you two. You always will have a home here, if you decide to come back."

"Thank you," Magdalys said.

"Oh, and here." She held an envelope out to Amaya. "I got this from Von Marsh's purse for you, the night of the riots."

Amaya just stared at her.

"It's the gram. From your father."

"I know what it is," Amaya said. "I just . . ." She blinked, and for a few seconds, Magdalys wasn't sure if her friend was about to burst out crying or break out into a huge smile. Finally, she let out a long breath and then took the gram from Marietta. "Thank you." She shoved it into her bag and walked over to the pteranodon without another word.

Cymbeline and Halsey made their way through the group of adults gathered to say goodbye.

Halsey stepped up first. "You are a rare flower, Miss Magdalys. And you know I mean that because it's not a quote, but straight from my heart to yours."

Magdalys smiled and accepted his way-too-firm handshake. "Please take care of yourself, Mr. Crunk. We need your voice lighting up the world."

He looked startled, blinked away some tears, and nodded, stepping back.

"I'm going to miss you," Magdalys said when Cymbeline came forward.

"Miss me? Girl, what are you talking about? I'm coming with you too!"

Magdalys laughed. "You're . . . Wait, you're serious?"

"You think I just brought this bag of clothes and my shotgun up on the roof for fun?"

With all the excitement and goodbyes, Magdalys hadn't

even noticed that Cymbeline was fully packed and ready for travel. "You're serious!"

"Of course! I can't let you roll down into the middle of a war without me. I was literally born for this."

They both laughed.

"And anyway, you'll need some entertainment along the way. It's a long trip, and Two Step and Mapper only know so many bad jokes."

"Hey!" they both yelled from the saddle.

Magdalys didn't know what to say, so she just stepped out of the way so Cymbeline could load up her things and climb on.

Halsey had clearly already said goodbye to his sister. He smiled sadly, watching her walk off, and muttered, "Once more unto the breach, dear friends, once more."

Magdalys took one last look over the tumbling rooftops of Dactyl Hill, Brooklyn — it was the one place she'd truly thought of as home, and she'd only lived there a couple of days.

But home, she realized, hoisting herself onto the saddle and smiling at the roiling banter of her friends behind her, was something she would have to take with her everywhere she went.

With a magnificent caw, Stella spread her wings and took off, launching out across the gathering morning over Brooklyn and heading south toward Montez, south toward the slaver states and the bristling battle lines, south toward war.

A NOTE ON THE PEOPLE, PLACES & DINOS OF THE DACTYL HILL SQUAD

Let me get this out of the way right off the bat: **There were no dinosaurs during the Civil War era!** In fact, there were no dinosaurs at any point in time during human history. The Dactyl Hill Squad series is historical fantasy. That means it's based on an actual time and place, events that actually happened, but I also get to make up awesome stuff, like that there were dinosaurs running around. So some of the people, places, and events are based on real historical facts, some are inspired by real historical facts, and some are just totally made up. Throughout this note, I've given some recommendations on books that helped me pull all this together; some of them were written for adult readers, so make sure they're the right ones for you before diving in.

PEOPLE!

Magdalys Roca and the other orphans are not based on any specific people, but there was indeed a Colored Orphan Asylum, and their records speak of a family of kids mysteriously dropped off from Cuba without much explanation. That was part of the inspiration behind this book. You can read those stories and more about the Colored Orphan Asylum in Leslie Harris's book *In the Shadow of Slavery*.

Halsey and Cymbeline Crunk are inspired by Ira Aldridge and James Hewlett, two early black Shakespearean actors who performed in New York City. Hewlett cofounded the African Grove Theater, the first all-black Shakespearean troupe in the United States. Richard III was one of Hewlett's signature performances, and he did indeed revel in audience participation and adjust the language in the plays to speak directly to his crowd, which consisted mainly of his fellow black New Yorkers (he even added the word *New* before *York* in Richard's opening monologue, as Halsey Crunk does at the Bochinche). Hewlett's troupe performed in New York during the 1830s, about thirty years before the Dactyl Hill Squad series takes place. Like the Zanzibar, the Grove was burned down in what was probably a racist attack, and Hewlett sought friendlier audiences overseas in Europe and later in Trinidad. But besides those similarities, Halsey and Cymbeline Crunk are entirely made-up characters. You can read more about Hewlett in Shane White's book *Stories of Freedom in Black New York.*

David Ballantine is also a fictional character, but he's one inspired by the real-life organizer and abolitionist David Ruggles. Mr. Ruggles founded and led the Vigilance Committee, which functioned essentially like the version in this book (minus the dinosaurs): They would intervene in the unlawful detainment of refugees from slavery and free black New Yorkers and keep them from being sent south to slavery. Ruggles eventually ended up in Florence, Massachusetts, and had died by the time this book takes place, but the Vigilance Committee kept up its work, making New York a crucial stopping point along the Underground Railroad right up into the 1860s.

Louis Napoleon really did work with different organizations, including the Vigilance Committee, to make sure refugees from the slaver states made it in and out of New York safely, often meeting them at the train station or docks and escorting them to a designated safe house. He was illiterate but still managed to secure necessary documents from the court system to protect his charges from being recaptured. You can read more about him in *Gateway to Freedom* by Eric Foner.

Richard Riker was a real-life magistrate in the New York City courts, and he did indeed run an organization called the Kidnapping Club that captured black New Yorkers and sent them into slavery, often without a trial or due process. The infamous Rikers Island prison is not named after him, although you'd think it would be. Whether or not he was skilled at raptor riding is unknown.

Redd is one of my favorite characters in the book and I wish he actually existed, but he's not based on any real-life figures. He does appear as a spirit in modern-day Brooklyn in one of my books for adults, *Battle Hill Bolero,* the final novel in the Bone Street Rumba series.

Dr. James McCune Smith was both a doctor and abolitionist who worked closely with the American Anti-Slavery Society and the Colored Orphan Asylum.

Frederick Douglass was born into slavery and escaped, eventually rising to become one of the most noted anti-slavery activists in the world. Two of his sons served as soldiers during the Civil War.

Mr. Calloway, Miss Bernice, and Miss Josephine Du Monde are all totally made up.

PLACES & EVENTS

Dactyl Hill is based on a real historical neighborhood in Brooklyn called Crow Hill (modern-day Crown Heights), which, along with Weeksville and several others, became a safe haven for black New Yorkers escaping the racist violence of Manhattan. You can find out more about Weeksville at the Weeksville Historical Society and in Judith Wellman's book *Brooklyn's Promised Land.*

The **Dactyl Hill Penitentiary** is based on the Kings County Penitentiary, which sat at the top of Crow Hill on Kingston Avenue and President Street. It was torn down in 1910.

The **bone factory** was a real spot in Crow Hill where they created fertilizer from ground-up animal bones. This was rumored to be the source of all the crows that gave the neighborhood its name. There is no indication that it housed a giant pterosaur.

The **Bochinche** is a totally made-up hangout spot. But if it existed I would definitely hang out there!

The **Spine Islands** don't exist in real life, although there are lots of cool little islands in New York Harbor. You can also read more about the fictional Spine Islands in *Battle Hill Bolero*.

Vigilance Committee Headquarters really was at 32 Lispenard Street, and you can see a plaque on that building today commemorating their work and the leadership of David Ruggles. They had mostly ceased operations by the time of the Civil War.

The **Colored Orphan Asylum** was on Fifth Avenue between Forty-Second and Forty-Third Streets in Manhattan. It was burned down in the New York Draft Riots. All the orphans except one escaped, and the organization relocated to another building.

The **Zanzibar Savannah Theater** is based on Hewlett's African Grove Theater, home of the first all-black Shakespearean acting company in the United States. It was burned down in 1836.

In July 1863, when this book takes place, the Union Army had just achieved two major and decisive victories after two and a half years of the **Civil War**. At Gettysburg, the newly promoted General Meade repelled General Lee's Army of Northern Virginia, effectively ending the Confederate invasion of Pennsylvania; and in Mississippi, General Grant sacked the fortress city of Vicksburg after a prolonged siege. Starting earlier that same year, the US government finally allowed black soldiers to be mustered into service, although they insisted on paying them significantly less than their white counterparts. From Maine to the Midwest all the way down to Louisiana, many thousands answered the call anyway. Besides fighting valiantly in combat, they agitated successfully for equal pay, and eventually made up 10 percent of the Union Army. You can read more about the famed Massachusetts 54th and 55th regiments in *Thunder at the Gates* by Douglas R. Egerton. *A History of the Negro Troops in the War of the Rebellion, 1861–1865* is also a fascinating historical overview written twenty years after the war by a former soldier and one of the first African American historians, George Washington Williams. There are numerous other books about the Civil War, but one of the best is *Battle Cry of Freedom* by James McPherson.

The **Battle of Milliken's Bend**, which Montez was wounded in, was indeed a decisive moment in the victory at Vicksburg, as the 9th Louisiana Regiment of African Descent and others repelled an attempt by the Confederates to reinforce their besieged troops.

The **New York Draft Riots** took place in July 1863, when coordinated mobs attacked various draft houses, armories, and black businesses in Manhattan. While the riots were in response to a law enacting the draft, much of the violence was directed at black New Yorkers, a number of whom were killed. As a result, many of the survivors fled to Brooklyn. The actual Draft Riots took place on July 13–16, a week after Gettysburg and the fall of Vicksburg and the events of this book.

The **Golden Circle** was a planned expansion of the slaver states into the Caribbean and Central and South America. The Knights of the Golden Circle were comprised of various pro-slavery advocates throughout the Americas who were dedicated to bringing their plan to fruition.

The ***Ocarrion*** is a made-up boat, but there was indeed a famous case where a group of black New Yorkers took over a Brazilian slave ship in New York Harbor and freed the enslaved people on board. In a similar incident, David Ruggles boarded a slave ship and personally apprehended the captain, bringing him before the court in a much-publicized case.

DINOS, PTEROS & OTHER ASSORTED -SAURIA

For obvious reasons, a lot less is known about dinosaurs than about Civil War–era New York. Because of this, and because this is a fantasy novel, I took more liberties with the creation of the dinosaurs in this story than I did with the history. Experts can make intelligent guesses based on the fossil data, but we don't really know exactly what prehistoric animals looked like, smelled like, or how they acted. In the world of Dactyl Hill Squad, the dinos never went extinct, but humans did subdue and domesticate them as beasts of burden and war.

The **brachiosaurus** was a humongous herbivorous (meaning it ate plants) quadruped (meaning it walked on four legs). Its long neck allowed it to eat leaves from the tallest trees. It lived during the Late Jurassic Period and probably didn't hoot the way the ones in the Dactyl Hill Squad world do.

Sauropod is a general term for the gigantic quadrupedal dinosaurs with long necks, long tails, and relatively small heads. In the Dactyl Hill Squad world, they are used for transportation, cargo carrying, and construction.

As Magdalys points out, **pterodactyls** weren't dinosaurs, they were pterosaurs, flying reptiles closely related to birds. They flew through Jurassic–era skies munching on insects, fish, and small reptiles. Generally about the size of seagulls, they weren't really large enough to carry a person. A group of pterodactyls is not called a squad (although maybe it should be!) and scientists don't suspect them to have been pack dependent as described in the book. But who knows?

Raptors were a group of intelligent, bipedal (meaning they walked on two feet) carnivores (meaning they ate meat). They had rod-straight tails and a giant claw on each foot, and they hunted in packs during the Late Cretaceous Period.

Like pterodactyls, **mosasauruses** weren't dinosaurs. They were mosasaurs, a group of large aquatic (meaning they lived in the water) reptiles that roamed the oceans in the Late Cretaceous Period. Fierce hunters with giant heads, they grew to be fifty feet long — bigger than a T. rex!

Triceratopses were herbivorous quadrupeds about the size of an ice cream truck that roamed the earth during the Late Cretaceous Period. They had three horns: one protruding from the snout and two longer ones that stuck out from a wide shield over their eyes that stretched out over their neck.

Ankylosaurs were armor-backed dinos of the Late Cretaceous Period. They probably didn't move quite as fast as the ones in the world of Dactyl Hill Squad do, which may have made it easier to fire a musket while riding one.

The **tyrannosaurus** is probably the most famous of the dinosaurs. It lived during the Late Cretaceous Period in western North America and was known as the king of dinos. It was bipedal, carnivorous, and about as long as a school bus.

Pteranodons were large, mostly toothless pterosaurs without long tails. In fact, their name means "toothless lizard." Quetzalcoatlus, the largest of pterosaurs, was as big as a fighter plane — forty-five feet long. They ruled the skies of the Late Cretaceous Period.

Pachycephalosaurs ("thick head"), known here as **knuckleskulls,** were bipedal herbivores that lived during the Late Cretaceous Period. They ranged from the size of small dogs to fifteen feet long and their skulls were as thick as bowling balls.

Plesiosaurs were giant fish-eating ocean reptiles of the dinosaur age. They had long slender necks and four big paddle-shaped flippers. The largest of them grew to nearly fifty feet long.

A NOTE ON WEAPONS & WORDS

In this messy, broken time of mass shootings and state violence, it's important to note that guns almost always create more problems than they solve. More than that: Young people suffer with trauma from those problems in increasing and heartbreaking numbers. This is an adventure story, and it takes place during a war, in an era when folks were being kidnapped and sold into slavery and an invading rebel army threatened the nation's capital. Guns are one of the parts of life in the time that I chose to include in this story, but I hope that a) the dangers, both physical and emotional, of gun violence ring loud and clear on the page, and b) we one day live in a time when gun violence doesn't exist anymore at all.

WEAPONS

Flintlock pistols were hard to load: You had to put gunpowder in the muzzle along with the bullet, shove it in with something called a ramrod, and then put some more black powder in a little chamber near the trigger, pull back the hammer (which had a little piece of flint in it, hence the name), thus cocking the gun, and finally fire, which would result in a big smoky explosion. Whew! That's a lot of work for one shot. Soldiers in the Revolutionary War used flintlock pistols and muskets. By the time of the Civil War, most people had upgraded their flintlocks to a much speedier mechanism called a caplock, but there were still a few around.

Cymbeline's favorite weapon, the **double-barrel shotgun**, was for the most part a civilian weapon in the 1860s, meaning that it was not an official military-issued gun, although some soldiers did carry them into the Civil War battlefields. It is generally a smoothbore gun, meaning that the inside of the barrel is smooth, not rifled (a process that makes ridged spirals in the barrel and increases aiming capabilities.) The shotgun is a short-range weapon, and usually fires a bunch of small projectiles called shot or a single one called a slug.

A **blunderbuss** is a clunky old ancestor of the shotgun. It's a smoothbore and has a short barrel that widens at the muzzle. That wide muzzle is where you would put the slug or shot in, which is why it's called a muzzle-loading firearm.

Rifled muskets are enhanced versions of the old Revolutionary War firearms. The rifled muzzles gave these weapons greater precision, and their caplock mechanisms made them easier to load and fire than their flintlock ancestors. Rifled muskets, both Enfields and Springfields, were the most commonly issued guns on both sides of the Civil War.

Many rifled muskets were armed with a **bayonet,** a sharpened sword attached to the muzzle that could be used to stab an attacker.

The **carbine** is smaller and lighter than the rifled musket, with a shorter barrel. Because they are breach-loading, meaning you insert the bullets at the middle of the gun instead of into the muzzle, they are easier to shoot from horseback (or dinoback) and thus were favored by cavalry (mounted) units.

A **cutlass** is a short, broad sword that usually had a sharpened cutting edge used for slashing. The handle often had a protective basket guard around it. The cutlass was a favorite sword of pirates.

The **howitzer** is a short-barreled smoothbore mobile artillery cannon that could fire shells of twelve, twenty-four, and thirty-two pounds in a high trajectory. They were used as defensive weapons and to flush enemies out of their entrenched hiding places.

WORDS

Besides taking the liberty of adding dinos to nineteenth-century American history, I also gave myself a little bit of leeway with language. The characters of Dactyl Hill Squad don't speak much like what the actual folks in 1860s New York spoke like. I opted to go with more modern dialogue and lingo, in part because I didn't want their conversations to be distracting and feel distant. However, I did keep a few slang words of the era in the book.

Here's a list of some cool gangster slang from the streets of nineteenth-century New York (compiled from the book *The Rogue's Lexicon*, by George W. Matsell):

arch coves: *n.*, chief of a gang. Headman. Governor.

ballum rancum: *n.*, a ball where all the attendees are members of the gangster community.

bandog: *n.*, civil officer. Cop.

Billy Noodle: *n.*, a fool that thinks he's a ladies' man.

bracket mug: *adj.*, irredeemably ugly.

cocum: *adj.*, sly, wary.

crosleite: *v.*, cheating a friend.

cull: *n.*, man.

drab: *n.*, mean woman.

flash your ivory: *idiom*; smile.

hickjop: *n.*, a fool.

hobinol: *n.*, a clown.

jazey: *n.*, unnecessarily hairy man.

jinglebrains: *n.*, someone who acts recklessly without thinking.

looby: *n.*, a fool.

moose-face: *n.*, a rich but ugly man.

nocky boy: *n.*, an obtuse male child.

scrobe: *v.*, to chastise privately.

stow your whid: *idiom*; shut up.

For more information on criminal life in old New York, check *The Gangs of New York* by Herbert Asbury.

ACKNOWLEDGMENTS

This book, more than any other I've written, has felt like it really did take a squad to make happen. Of course! First and foremost, I am deeply grateful to Nick Thomas and Weslie Turner — I could not ask for two more brilliant editors. You are both gifts.

Thank you to the whole team at Scholastic, who have been amazing throughout this process, especially Arthur A. Levine, Lizette Serrano, Emily Heddleson, Tracy van Straaten, Rachel Feld, Isa Caban, and Erik Ryle.

As soon as this project became a reality, I wanted Nilah Magruder to do the art for it, so working with her has been an actual-factual dream come true. She brings Magdalys and the crew to life with so much verve and excellence. I am so grateful. A huge thank you also to Afu Chan for the absolutely terrific

Dactyl Hill Squad logo and to the unstoppable Christopher Stengel for bringing it all together, as always, magnificently.

To Eddie Schneider and Joshua Bilmes and the whole team at JABberwocky Lit: you are awesome. Thank you.

Many thanks to Leslie Shipman at the Shipman Agency and Lia Chan at ICM. Thanks to Chris Myers for planting the idea of writing a Middle Grade fantasy in my imagination as we shared a taxi downtown one afternoon.

Thank you to my wonderful beta readers: Leigh Bardugo, Laurie Halse Anderson, Nic Stone, Brittany Nicole Williams, Adisa Terry (who at twelve years old gave some of the best notes I've gotten), and Darcie Little Badger. Huge thanks to Kortney Ziegler at Black Star Media for his wisdom and thoughts about Redd. Thanks to Sorahya Moore for being a wonderful mentee and friend and curating the list of great old-time slang at the end.

Besides writing one of the books that inspired this story, *In the Shadow of Slavery*, Leslie Harris was also kind enough to provide her insight on early drafts of *Dactyl Hill Squad* and I am so grateful. I also want to thank Shane White and Barnet Shecter, for their historical expertise, and Don Lessem for his help with the dinos. All incorrect historical or dinofactual matter is my own fault and it's probably on purpose, unless it's in the appendix and then it's totally my bad. Either way, don't try any of this at home.

Thanks always to my amazing family, Dora, Marc, Malka, Lou, Calyx, and Paz. Thanks to Iya Lisa and Iya Ramona and

Iyalocha Tima, Patrice, Emani, Darrell, April, and my whole Ile Omi Toki family for their support; also thanks to Oba Nelson "Poppy" Rodriguez, Baba Craig, Baba Malik, Mama Akissi, Mama Joan, Sam, Tina, Jud, and all the wonderful folks of Ile Ase. And thank you, Brittany, for everything.

I give thanks to all those who came before us and lit the way. I give thanks to all my ancestors; to Yemonja, Mother of Waters; gbogbo Orisa, and Olodumare.

ABOUT THE AUTHOR

Daniel José Older has always loved monsters, whether historical, prehistorical, or imaginary. His debut series for young adults, the Shadowshaper Cypher, has earned starred reviews, the International Latino Book Award, and *New York Times* Notable Book and NPR Best Books of the Year picks, among other accolades. His books for adults include *Star Wars: Last Shot*, the Bone Street Rumba urban fantasy series, and *The Book of Lost Saints*. He has worked as a bike messenger, a waiter, a teacher, and was a New York City paramedic for ten years. Daniel splits his time between Brooklyn and New Orleans. You can find out more about him at danieljoseolder.net.

READ ON FOR A SNEAK PEEK OF
MAGDALYS AND THE SQUAD'S NEXT
THRILLING ADVENTURE IN...

BOOK TWO

"What is it?" Two Step asked.

"Something's coming," Magdalys said, backing toward the trees. "Can't make it out." The shapes got closer. There were three of them and they were tall and very fast. "Run! Get to the woods!"

A shot cracked through the night and Magdalys almost crumpled into herself from surprise. It was Amaya, she realized. Out in the field, a dino squealed and someone yelled, "Ho, there!"

"Hold your fire," Cymbeline called. "Get into the woods!"

Magdalys and Amaya backed into the shadows of the trees together, guns pointed out at the approaching riders. Cymbeline stepped forward, a lit lantern raised above her head, shotgun in the other hand. "Declare yourselves!" she hollered. "Or get annihilated."

"Whoa, there, whoa," a low voice muttered in a long Tennessee drawl as the riders dismounted and stepped forward. "Almost winged Horace." In the dim lantern light, Magdalys could make out their faces. All three men sported beards trimmed to line their jaws with no mustaches. And, except for a long scar running down the man in the center's cheek, all three had exactly the same face. Worse than that, they wore the gray uniforms of Confederate cavalrymen. Magdalys gasped.

"Card!" Cymbeline said, shaking her head and laughing. "It's about time! Where have you been?"

"Cymbeline!" the whole Dactyl Hill Squad gaped at the same time.

"You . . . you . . ." Magdalys stuttered. On the other side of Cymbeline, Amaya raised the carbine, her face steel.

Cymbeline shook her head. "No, wait, slow down everyone! I see what this looks like, and it's not . . ." She sighed. "They're not Confederates, okay?"

"Then why . . ." Two Step demanded, waving his arms in exasperated, self-explanatory little circles. "Why!"

The man in the middle smirked. "You can see why they might think we were though, Cymbie."

"Card is a Union scout," Cymbeline said. "He goes behind enemy lines to find out their positions and —"

"We know what a scout does," Mapper seethed.

"Then you can understand why he's dressed like that."

Magdalys felt like all the blood in her body was rushing into her brain. This whole situation was rotten, from the moment Cymbeline had said they should land onward.

"What I want to know, Cymbeline, is how did they know where we were going to be and why were you expecting them?"

This book was edited by
Nick Thomas and Weslie Turner and
designed by Christopher Stengel. The production
was supervised by Rachel Gluckstern. The text was set
in Adobe Caslon Pro, with display type set in Brothers. The
book was printed and bound at LSC Communications
in Crawfordsville, Indiana. The manufacturing
was supervised by Angelique Browne.

New Jersey
HUDSON RIVER
DINOFEED WAREHOUSE DISTRICT
DUMPING GROUNDS
Manhattan
Vigilance Committee Headquarters
Colored Orphan Asylum
Zanzibar Theater
Weed's House
Ferry Port to Breuklyn
THE STINKPIT
THE RAPTOR CLAW
EAST RIVER
Brooklyn
SPINE ISLANDS
DOWNTOWN BROOKLYN
RED HOOK
Flatbush Ave.
Atlantic Ave.
THE CREST
WEEKSVILLE
DACTYL HILL